Her Every Wish

Courtney Milan

For a dog named Lucky.
I wish you were around to hate this book.

Chapter 1

London, England, November, 1866

The crowd stood elbow to elbow, buffeting Daisy Whitlaw about as if she were a slice of bread that had landed in a bucket of slops. No wonder; she suspected she was about to be thrown to the pigs.

A temporary stage had been set up in the square just outside the church. A few dead leaves lay in the gutter as a reminder of autumn, but the trees were bare. The days were growing shorter and colder, but the holidays were too far away to seem real. Perhaps that was why the awarding of the charity bequest felt like such a celebration.

Wooden benches ringed the stage, but nobody was sitting. It was cold, and sitting was freezing work. People shifted from foot to foot, chafing gloved hands, leaning in close to one another. The crowd on this fine Saturday afternoon was jovial. They'd worked their half-day. Most of them had already downed a pint or seven of their favorite ale, and the afternoon's entertainment still lay ahead of them.

Daisy gritted her teeth and popped up on her toes. She still couldn't see.

"Excuse me." She tapped the shoulder of the big, broad fellow who was blocking her view.

He didn't notice her. She was used to this. With a sigh, Daisy jumped atop the bench. From this vantage point, she could see over the man's head. She was five rows back. Close enough, she hoped. Gray buildings enclosed the square, the walls high and grim in the dying light. The noise from the docks was a distant, ever-present roar, layering over the hum of the crowd.

More importantly, the respected, gray-bearded grocer who had been appointed to run the proceedings was already standing at the podium. They were about to start.

Daisy knew she didn't have a chance. She'd been foolish to enter. Still, she'd done it, and there was no walking away now.

"All right, you lot," the grocer at the front bellowed. He was grinning, too, his face flushed with what was undoubtedly more than his fair share of beer. "You all know what we're here for, so let's get started. Sit down, everyone, sit down."

There was a general rumble. The man in front of Daisy started to sit on her feet without looking behind him; she yelped and jumped off the bench, scarcely in time. There was one spot on the end of the row. Daisy slipped into it just ahead of another woman, who gave her a cheerful shrug before retreating farther back.

"We're here," the grocer said as the crowd's noise subsided to a mere rumble, "to settle the terms of the late Mr. and Mrs. Wilding's bequest. They've left fifty pounds to be given to one promising individual who attends services at St. Peter's."

"Hear, hear!" called someone in the crowd.

The grocer paused for a nod at the vicar before continuing. "In the month since the initial announcement, we've received proposals of business from forty-seven young people, all of whom wish to start a trade."

Daisy had her letter of acceptance in her skirt pocket. She'd scarcely believed her luck when it had arrived. Good news rarely came her way. Letters came from creditors, not charity committees.

But she'd labored over her proposal. Every spare hour she had, and then some, had gone into it. She couldn't fail now.

She folded her hands in front of her as the crowd slowly quieted. A ridiculous figure of speech, that. A stupid one. Clearly, she *could* fail now. Failure was expected. Failure was a given.

Every time she reached for her dreams, someone slapped her hands away. Still, she kept on reaching. She wouldn't have the best proposal; she knew it. Men who had studied business had no doubt entered. She didn't know why she kept trying. She just knew that she did.

"We've selected the ten finest proposals that were put before us," the grocer was saying. "Those ten promising young people will deliver a preliminary description of the business they wish to enter today. Each of the five judges will choose the best of this lot. Seven days hence, we'll hear their perfected proposals. The most promising one will receive the full fifty pounds."

That was what the bequest had said. Daisy had read the announcement posted on the church wall over and over to be certain. *The most promising proposal.* Not, *the* man *with the most promising proposal.*

Daisy's position at the flower shop was secure— assuming Mr. Trigard, the owner, didn't hear about this little excursion on her part. With the little extra her mother earned for her lacework, they made do.

She wasn't starving. She had no reason to enter this competition. None, except that she hoped to win.

"And so, without any further ado," the grocer declaimed, "I should like to invite our first candidate up to present his proposal. Mr. J. Batting, please come up."

The crowd applauded, and a man near Daisy let out a sharp whistle. Daisy knew Jonathan Batting. He was the blacksmith's second son, about three years her elder. He lumbered up to the stage and started explaining the plan he had for a new business making straight pins.

She'd expected something stupendous from him. Pins? Factories made straight pins these days, and in far greater quantity, at far lower cost, than any individual man could manage. But the judges nodded gravely as Batting spoke. They asked how he would compete with factory goods.

"Quality," Batting said, with the placid intellect of a cow contemplating its cud. "I'll deliver superior quality."

Superior-quality pins. Had there been any chance anyone preferred handmade straight pins, pin factories would not have driven pin-makers to the poorhouse. Daisy shook her head. She wouldn't win, but maybe her chances weren't so terrible.

Mr. Edwin Diggle spoke about his proposed business as a copyist. Mr. Allan Ebler had a plan to sell fish from a cart. Mr. Arden Flisk intended to own a dry-goods store. He'd need more than fifty pounds to amass a creditable store of dry goods—had nobody done any research? By the time the judges had worked through Misters Glowter, Hargo, Manning, Porget, and Walder on their way down the alphabet to Whitlaw, Daisy was beginning to feel an unreal sense of hope. *None* of the ideas were as good as hers. They wouldn't toss her out, even though she was—

"Our final candidate. D. Whitlaw," the grocer announced. "Mr. D. Whitlaw, if you will."

Daisy stood and started up the aisle.

The grocer frowned and scanned the crowd. "Mr. D. Whitlaw? Is Mr. D. Whitlaw here?"

Daisy drew in a deep breath. "Sir." It came out a squeak.

He glanced at her down his nose and looked away. In that moment, she saw herself as he must see her: skinny, pale, almost ghostlike, standing in the aisle. Her best gown was dark brown. Once, the flowers imprinted on the cotton had been yellow. Now they might charitably be described as beige.

She'd let out the hem as far as it would go. It went…not quite far enough. That extra black stripe at her ankles proclaimed that this was a gown she'd made over and over again. Daisy's Sunday finest was much like her hopes: worn to threadbare weariness, not quite dire enough to be discarded.

"David Whitlaw?" the grocer asked hopefully. "Or maybe Damien? Darius? Daniel?"

"Sir." Daisy spoke a little more loudly. "Sir. I am D. Whitlaw."

The grocer frowned at her, his eyes shifting away, then returning. He rubbed his forehead. He adjusted his spectacles, squinting in her direction. Finally he spoke. "Is the entrant your brother? I hope he's not ill. The rules are that he must speak on his behalf in person."

She squared her shoulders and raised herself up to her full height. "Sir," she repeated. "I am D. Whitlaw. D is for Daisy."

He stared at her in utter confusion, as if she were a fish who had announced her intention to stand for Parliament. Behind her, she heard a high titter of amusement.

"You." He licked his lips. "Where's your brother?"

"I don't have a brother." Daisy raised her voice as loud as it would go. "I'm D. Whitlaw. I'm the tenth candidate."

The frown on the man's face intensified. "But you're a woman."

"The bequest is for the best proposal." Daisy stood ramrod straight, clasping her hands behind her back. "Not for the man with the best proposal. I have a proposal."

The grocer pulled back a step. "Manhood is generally understood to be a prerequisite. The bequest is assumed to be for a man."

Daisy stood in place, refusing to leave. She'd planned out an argument, something about the law and presumptions and whatnot. Now, with him glaring at her, she felt her throat go dry. Her argument evaporated.

She had no words any longer. She felt ungainly, unwanted. Everyone was watching her. She should just sit down and apologize.

Her legs wouldn't move.

The grocer's lip curled. "Feisty, are you?"

Cats were feisty. The word he was looking for was *hopeful*. Perhaps *unrealistic*. Daisy didn't say anything. She stood stock still, looking at him.

He sighed. "Well, I suppose it's the thing these days for women to ape men. We shouldn't be surprised that it's happening here. What do you say, gentlemen? Shall we give *Miss Daisy Whitlaw* the chance to show how women compare to men?"

Nine men to one woman. The odds were entirely unfair. They were also no worse than any Daisy had faced in the past.

"Come on up, then," the grocer said with a smile that was definitely not kind.

She ascended the steps, her knees stiff with the effort of not knocking together. It felt very cold on that high platform. Without the crowd to shield her, the wind seemed to slice through the fabric of her gown. Still, she marched to the front where the other candidates had stood.

"Tell me," the grocer said with a smirk. "Tell us all what sort of trade a woman wants to engage in."

"I'll take her in trade!" shouted a man from the back.

Daisy looked over the gathering and swallowed back an exclamation.

As a single member of the crowd, the people around her had seemed an overwhelming sea of indifferent waves. Even when she'd addressed the grocer, she'd not had to look at anyone else. But now she stood in front, and every face was turned to her. The gathering felt hostile. All those eyes bored into her. Every person seemed to murmur to one another.

She imagined their whispered conversations. *Look at that stupid girl. She'll come in dead last.*

She started speaking anyway. "We have fish carts. We have flower shops. We even have copyists. We don't need any more of them."

People stared at her in sullen disapproval.

"We don't have any of what I propose." Daisy had practiced her speech often enough that she could launch into it despite the dryness of her mouth. "Daisy's Emporium will be a small shop of carefully selected goods. Durable, beautiful, and inexpensive. Designed for—" *Women,* she had been going to say, but she was speaking too fast. And looking out over those disapproving faces…

They didn't want to hear about women and their wants.

She inhaled. "I propose a business in a central location, one where—"

"Speak up, girl," the grocer said. "Nobody can hear you."

She tried again a little more loudly. "I propose a business in a central location, one—"

"Can anyone hear the girl?" the grocer asked.

"Yes!" shouted a man in the back.

"Because all I hear," he said, "is something like the squeaking of a mouse."

Daisy's face flushed hot. She turned to him. "*I propose a business in a central location,*" she bellowed at the top of her lungs. "*One that provides inexpensive items designed to lift spirits, beautify homes, and teach relevant skills.*"

The grocer looked upward. "How like a woman. Screaming like a fishwife already."

She was not going to let him bait her. Daisy took a deep breath and recalled her place in her memorized speech. "The cost of all this—"

"Oh dear," the grocer said. "Please stop before you get into the figures. We know what happens when women attempt mathematics."

"I have to do the figures." She could not keep the hopelessness out of her voice. "It's part of the bequest." She turned back to the crowd and tried to put on a smile. But if that mass of faces had looked unfriendly before, it seemed downright hostile now.

"The cost of all this," she made herself say, "is, as an initial outlay, fifteen pounds per annum in rents as determined by…" She was stumbling now, the words she'd practiced so many times sounding rote and boring. The people in the back could no longer hear her; they were turning away.

A man at the back stood. At first she thought he was going to leave. Instead, he stepped into the aisle and hurled something at her. She watched the brown blob come sailing in her direction, watched it in confusion, scarcely able to move away as it hurtled toward her. She stepped aside just as it landed on the wooden platform with a disheartening plop.

Horse dung.

It took the words right out of her mouth. She looked at the man. He smiled at her, a cruel, ugly smile.

Before she had a chance to say anything, another man materialized at his side. The new fellow took the man by the elbow and spun him around lightly. She could only tell that he'd wrenched the man's arm by the sudden squeal the thrower let out.

The newcomer leaned down, whispered something in the man's ear, and then pushed him to the ground before raising his face to Daisy.

She'd known who it was from the moment he had stood. Crash stood out in any crowd. It wasn't just the color of his skin—a pale brown—nor the brightness of his smile. He had an air about him, one that always attracted attention.

"Go on, Daisy." Those were the words she thought his mouth formed. Or maybe he'd said, "Go to hell, Daisy." Either was equally likely from him.

Once, she'd loved Crash's attention. Every moment he'd given her. Every wicked smile. Once, she'd believed that…

But none of her wishes ever came true. It wasn't fair, but it was her life, and she was used to it.

"So." She swallowed. "These are the figures." She'd spent so long gathering them; now she felt herself deflating like a child's broken toy. She stumbled through the end of her speech.

Nobody applauded her.

"Well," the grocer said. "The men have presented their ideas. The woman has…tried. Now the judges will confer. They will each pick one candidate to advance to the final proceedings."

Daisy was left standing stupidly on the stage.

The grocer looked at her. "Go join your fellow…ah, candidates."

Daisy stumbled to the seats at the back of the stage.

None of the other men looked at her except Mr. Flisk, who turned around and whispered to her. "You took a spot from a man who might have needed it. A man with a family to support. You should be ashamed of yourself."

Oh, she was. What did you call someone who refused to learn? Who kept reaching above herself?

The judges stood one by one, coming to the front. "I choose Mr. Flisk," said the first judge. "Hargo," said another. They named Manning and Porget next.

They were the ones Daisy would have picked out of the proposals she had seen. She supposed that Mr. Diggle would be the last one chosen. Stupid or no, his proposal had been the most sound out of the remaining candidates.

The fifth judge came to the front. He didn't look at any of the candidates. He just looked out over the audience. He wouldn't choose her. Daisy knew it, the way she knew that snow was cold and winter turnips were bitter. She knew it in her chilled, numbing hands and her growling belly.

She'd reached. They'd slapped her down. It had happened to her often enough that she was almost used to it by now. One day, she'd learn to stop wasting effort chasing foolish dreams. One day. Just…not yet.

The final judge faced the crowd and said one word. "Whitlaw."

Daisy jumped. A well of hope started up inside her. There was a moment of utter silence from the crowd. Maybe the strain had finally driven her mad.

Maybe he hadn't said it. It couldn't be true.

But Mr. Flisk turned to look at her with venomous eyes. The crowd murmured more loudly.

"Well," the grocer managed after a meaningful pause. "We'll see you all next Saturday. And it looks like we have our entertainment in order. After all, we've just lined up the jester." He gave Daisy an exaggerated waggle of his eyebrows and let out a great, braying laugh, one that explained precisely why she'd been chosen.

Chapter 2

Daisy tried to sneak away.

It should have been easy; nobody would look at her, let alone talk to her. Yet somehow, the crowd seemed to have more elbows on the way out. People stepped in her way as if she were not present. Feet stamped on her own. And no apologies were made.

After she had the wind knocked out of her a third time by an "accidental" blow that nobody else seemed to notice, she gave up on fighting her way out of the square with the crowd. She simply waited, stamping her feet to keep them from freezing, until everyone had left.

Almost everyone. A small knot of women remained on the street corner, clustered in the growing darkness under an unlit lamp.

She didn't want to go past them. She knew who was at the center of that knot, knew it before she could see him. Before she heard his voice.

"I was wondering," one of the women was saying. "I have always so wanted to ask you..."

"Yes?" Daisy recognized Crash's voice, even though she couldn't see him through the crowd around him. It felt like a shock to hear him even after all these months apart.

A flush of heat—shame and excitement all mixed together—rushed through her. Speak of wishes gone awry.

"By all means," Crash said, "ask me anything you like."

The woman giggled, and Daisy felt a kind of sorry kinship for her fellow sufferer. She did her best to slink past the little gathering. That poor woman might have been a flirt, but Crash was an incorrigible charmer. He flirted with anyone and everyone who gave him the opportunity, men and women alike. Everyone had to learn not to play with fire in her own way, and Crash had been as good a place for Daisy to learn that lesson as any.

Enjoy the ride, Daisy wished the girl as she slipped past. *I hope your heart can withstand what comes after.*

"It's this," the woman said, wide-eyed. "What *are* you?"

Ah. Daisy felt a little less sorry for her. *That* had to be the worst way to flirt with Crash.

She caught a glimpse of him through the ring of women.

Crash took off his rounded hat and smoothed back black, lightly curled hair. Daisy had spent long enough staring at him to know that he looked like nobody she'd ever seen. In those heady months when she'd thought of nobody else, she'd spent a great deal of time looking at him, then at the rest of the world. Sailors, woodcuts of foreign delegations—it hadn't mattered. She'd searched for his features everywhere and found them only in him.

Those wide, dark eyes angled ever so slightly. His light brown skin never paled in winter. His hair never straightened. His cheeks took days to turn to patchwork stubble, which she knew only because he rarely bothered to shave.

"What am I? What sort of question is that?" She could imagine his smile—just a little tilted. "I should think that was clear enough."

Daisy ducked her head, proceeding down the steps. She couldn't help but glance at him as she slipped past.

"I am not a pineapple." He made a show of looking down his body, checking himself. Of course he drew attention to his own figure in the process. Crash was slim, lithe, and muscled. He had long fingers, slightly callused, square at their tips. Once, he'd held her…

She gave her head a shake and pointedly turned her face away.

But Crash was hard to ignore. "I am not an elephant, nor a mouse, nor an oak tree. I seem to land firmly in the human category."

"Yes, but…" The other woman's voice was trailing off behind Daisy. "What *sort* of human are you?"

"That much is apparent at one glance," Crash said. "I'm one hundred percent pure perfection. Now, if you'll excuse me?"

Daisy wouldn't look back. She wouldn't let him know she was paying attention.

"But—"

"Business calls," Crash said.

"But couldn't we—"

"I'm afraid not," she heard Crash saying.

"I haven't even said—"

She could just imagine the cocky smile Crash must be giving the woman. "It wouldn't have mattered," she heard him say. "Now run along."

Daisy could almost hear the sound of a heart breaking. She knew that sound all too well; she'd heard it in her own chest. She couldn't even really blame Crash for it; he'd done nothing but tell her the truth. It was her own fault that she'd wanted lies.

She didn't look behind her, but she could hear him following. "Excuse me," he said. "Pardon me."

There followed a set of gasps and a burst of applause. No doubt he'd done something ridiculous—something foolishly Crash-like, like doing a backflip off the steps to escape his hangers on.

She'd spent enough time watching him to know what he could do. She wasn't going to look. She wasn't.

"Daisy," Crash called behind her.

The word sounded like a warning. Once he'd said her name very differently, almost reverently. As if she were not some kind of joke. But she couldn't allow herself to dwell on that *once*. It wouldn't help.

The snow underfoot had changed from delicate white lace to the disgusting, dingy slush of well-trodden streets. Icy water seeped through the seams of her shoes. A cold wind tugged at her, and she cinched her scarf around her neck. She didn't look back. She wasn't foolish.

"Ahoy, Daisy."

She wouldn't turn. That little skirling breeze coming up behind her would make her eyes water, and she was not—she absolutely was *not*—going to let Crash see her cry. Not even if her tears were merely wind-induced.

But Crash had never been deterred by…well, anything, Daisy suspected. Certainly not anything so mild as someone purposefully failing to hear him. He came jogging up to her, settling into a walk at her side.

At least he wasn't on that terrible contraption he'd taken to riding about everywhere. What did he call that two-wheeled unbalanced monstrosity? A velocipede?

Ha. An accurate description; it made her think of some monstrous twenty-legged thing, rushing about. One of these days he was going to crack his skull when he fell from the dratted thing, and she…

She wasn't going to care when he killed himself, not one bit.

"Daisy," he said. "You rushed off far too soon."

She made the mistake of meeting his eyes. Crash was a man who had mastered the speaking glance. *This* one could have been an epic saga. It was the unshakeable look that a farm lad gave to his sweetheart when she was sentenced to be fed to a dragon. *Don't worry,* it promised. *I'll save you. I've a plan.*

It was the kind of look that would have that blushing farm girl spreading her legs for her love in the barn the night before she was condemned to die. She'd give up her virginity, her trust, her love, her future in one trembling hour. When she bid her swain farewell through tears and kisses, she would believe in her soul that he was going to kill the beast. She'd believe he would save her until the dragon crunched her between its teeth.

Even now, even knowing Crash as she did, a flush of heat blossomed along the back of her neck.

Daisy's mind knew all about Crash, even if her body pretended ignorance. She'd already given him everything. She'd had that trembling hour. All these months later, Daisy had no virginity, no trust, no love, and her future was chock-full of dragons.

"Aha," Crash said, coming to a temporary halt. He snapped his fingers. "Right. Of course. I forgot. I'm to address you as Miss Whitlaw now."

He gave her a teasing smile, arranged the cloth at his neck into a mockery of a cravat, and shifted his tone. When he spoke, he sounded almost proper—the way Daisy's mother sounded at her most querulous. The way Daisy spoke when she wanted people to take her seriously.

"My dear Miss Whitlaw," he said in that distinctive, plummy-sounding voice, "I know you've little desire to speak with me at the moment. But I have a business proposition to put before you."

"You may recall," Daisy said severely, "that I do not care for your line of business."

That smile on his face flickered. "My line of business is the business of making people happy."

Ha. "Yes," she said. "A great *many* people."

"A great many people," he agreed, instead of getting angry at her implication like a normal person would. "I'm here to offer my services."

"I had your services once," Daisy snapped. "I don't need them any longer."

"Services," Crash said with a slow grin. "Is that what we're calling it, now? It's a good thing you don't need them any *longer*. You couldn't find services any longer—or thicker—or harder than mine."

Her cheeks flamed in memory of *long* and *thick* and *hard*. "Crash. *Please* don't say things like that."

He shrugged. "It's simple. I saw what happened back there. They're planning to make a joke of you, you know. All they want is to laugh."

"I know," Daisy said through clenched teeth.

"You should give up now."

"I know." Her teeth ground against each other.

"But you won't."

He knew that, too. His knowing things about her had fooled her thoroughly. She'd thought she was special. She had thought he actually cared. She'd been such an idiot.

As these things are reckoned, you are a complete waste of a woman. That was what she had to remember him saying. Her teeth gritted.

"And since you won't give up," he said, "then you cannot leave them with one single thing to laugh at. You know that's how it works, yes?"

"I know," she whispered.

"You will have to be brilliant to win." He looked at her. "You won't be able to hesitate. You'll have to make them believe that nobody will be able to survive without your…" He frowned. "I couldn't actually hear. Your…emporium, was it?"

She was not about to be inveigled into a conversation with him.

"That means you will have to practice."

"I know all these things," Daisy muttered. "It doesn't matter. I'm not going to win."

"You'll need an audience to test yourself against," Crash continued on as if she hadn't spoken. "Not your friend the marchioness nor your mother. You need to practice in front of someone you hate. Someone who makes your stomach curdle. Someone who will ask questions while you want to smash his face in. If you can impress *that* man, you can impress anyone."

She frowned at him. "I'm not going to win."

"Aren't you?" He took off his hat and gave her a flourishing bow. "I am, as ever, at your service."

He straightened and set his hat back on his head at an angle that might have been called rakish. No, not rakish. Mere rakery was never good enough for Crash. He adjusted it to something altogether promiscuous.

Daisy eyed him suspiciously. "Stop flirting with me."

His eyes widened in *Who, me?* innocence.

"I'm not going to win. I have a sweetheart." She'd told him that before. She had nothing of the kind. But right now, a man—an honest man, a solid man, one with prospects and morals—seemed as good a talisman to hold up as any. She needed to remind herself why she'd cut ties with Crash.

"Of *course* you do," Crash said in a tone that dripped with treacly, disbelieving sincerity.

He had seen her just now. In public. He'd been the only one to stand up, such as it was, on her behalf. If Daisy had a sweetheart, he was the most delinquent, useless sweetheart in the existence of romantic entanglements. Either that, or...

"He's a sub-lieutenant in the Royal Navy," she invented. "He'll be promoted any day—in fact, I expect he's already been promoted, but you know how the mails are at conducting letters written overseas." She was saying too much. He would notice she was lying. "Once he's back in port, we'll marry. I'm not going to win. I don't *need* to win. And I certainly don't want your help."

Crash rolled his eyes. "Come now, Daisy. You should know me better than that. You think I offered to help you because I wanted to interfere with your sweetheart? Nothing could be further from the truth."

That sounded actually sincere, not overly so. She narrowed her eyes at him suspiciously. "What do you want, Crash? What do you really want?"

"Ooh." He scratched his chin. "So many things. Ten million pounds, a large house, three carriages—oh. Wait. You mean what do I want from *you?*"

She exhaled. "You're being obtuse."

"One of my greatest talents." Crash ducked his head as if she'd given him a compliment. As if she'd mentioned the only modest bone in his body. "I'm flattered that you realized. But you were asking me a question. What do I want with you?"

He looked up, and her skin prickled under his attention. It was just her luck that she was susceptible to him. To the dark entreaty of his eyes, the way he adjusted his hat on his head.

"What do I want with you?" He shrugged. "Come, Daisy. You know I take odds."

Among so many other things. If there was an occupation that skirted the edges of legality, Crash was involved in it. She'd seen him organize a spot of gambling at the slightest provocation. The bestowal of the charity bequest had turned into a pageant for the entire parish.

There might as well have been a banner floating over her head: *Place wagers here.*

Stupid to feel disappointment that he didn't want anything else from her. "I should have guessed. Of course you're gambling about the competition."

He reached into his pocket and took out the little book where she'd seen him record his bets. "Think on it, Daisy." He waved the leather-bound book at her before tucking it away. "After that little catastrophe on stage, do you imagine that *anyone* placed money that you would win? No. Everyone wanted to put odds on Hargo or Flisk. Imagine the purse I'd collect if you prevailed."

She let out an exhale. That was all she was to him at this point—a wager to be won. He looked at her and heard shillings rattling in his pockets.

"I'm going to win," she informed him.

"Aren't you?" His eyes bored into her. "The Daisy I once knew would never have said that."

She didn't want to be reminded of the person she had been. Gullible, naïve, and optimistic. She'd believed him when he said that he loved her as much as he breathed. That of course, had been *before* he took her virginity.

"As you are, you're not going to win. There's no chance of it. You need someone who will teach you how to swagger," he said in a low voice. "To ignore the shouted insults, the thrown horse droppings, and to shout out your confidence to the world. It's the only way you'll have a chance."

She folded her arms and glared at him.

He went on as if she'd issued an invitation for him to make a speech. "Make them believe that no matter how they posture, no matter how they bluster, you have nothing but victory in you."

Statements like that had drawn her to Crash. He could make the entire world disappear. He could make her forget how cold her feet were, how little money she had. She could look into his eyes and believe that she could prevail despite everything.

He was right. If she floundered about a week from now the way she had just now, she was not going to win.

She was not going to win with his help, either.

But some part of her, some foolish part, had never quite managed to give up all her naïve confidence. She had a brief vision of herself, standing on the stage in front of the crowd. Of the grocer calling her name as the winner.

She shoved it away.

She *wasn't* going to win, no matter what she did. But if she did her utmost... Maybe, maybe this time she'd finally learn not to waste her effort trying.

"Very well." Her voice came out a little too high. "I accept."

"An excellent choice. To us prevailing, then." He held out his hand as if he expected her to shake it.

She looked at his fingers. They were encased in wool gloves. She wouldn't have to touch his skin. She would scarcely even feel him. But she remembered too much about Crash, and *scarcely* was already too much.

Daisy put her hands behind her back. "No," she said. "No handshakes. There will be no touching of any kind. This is just business."

He gave her a sardonic smile. "We're nothing but business, you and I."

Her cheeks flamed and she turned away. Her legs could not move fast enough to get away from him and the memory his words sparked in her mind. Once, he had—

No. Absolutely not. She was *not* going to think of what she'd let Crash do.

"I'll see you Monday," he called after her. "At three, when I've done my rounds, outside the general store. You should be finished at the flower shop then, yes? Wear skirts that allow a good deal of movement."

She knew better than to let Crash get under her skin; really, she did. Still, she whipped around. "Don't talk about my skirts!" she hissed. "It's not proper."

He simply laughed.

God, what had she agreed to do?

Crash's aunt—and his uncle, when the man was in England—lived in a flat over a cooper's shop. At night, with all the customers departed and the apprentices off, the neighborhood was quiet. As quiet as anything ever was here, a quarter-mile from the eternal hum from the St. Katharine docks.

He stepped close to the door and detected the muted sounds of spirited voices.

His aunt had guests over. She often did; her husband was the first mate on a trading vessel, and in the months when he was away, she entertained.

He knocked and waited. The door opened, and a brilliant dazzle of light met him. For a moment, his aunt was nothing but a dark silhouette lit by the oil lamps from behind. Then she moved back a pace and the palette of her skin shifted from midnight to umber.

She tried, oh, she tried, to frown at him disapprovingly. Alas. His aunt was terrible at disapproval, particularly where he was involved.

He embraced her. "Aunt Ree."

She gave him a grudging pat on the back in return.

The other two women seated at the card table smiled at him over Ree's shoulder, as if the evening's entertainment had just arrived. Three white-haired women looking at him with that particular expression might have put another man off, but Crash knew them better.

Harriet Cathing had been his aunt's friend since before he was born. She'd been a laundress then, before she married a ship's lieutenant. Now she was… Well, technically, she was a laundress married to a ship's lieutenant.

May Walsh hadn't married anyone—at least not in a legally binding ceremony. She swore by the strategy to any of the young girls who would listen to her. She had a strong jaw and dark freckles spattering brown skin.

Once, Martha Claving had been the fourth whist player in their little quartet, and May's long-time partner and companion. A little pencil sketch in a black crepe-draped frame marked the place she would have taken.

His aunt was shaking her head at him. "Crash," she said, "Crash, Crash, Crash. You know Saturday night is whist night, and still you chose to invade. Ladies, you all know my scapegrace nephew. Crash, do try to be respectable."

It was a bit of a joke between them, that word.

Crash gave the gathering a sweeping bow. "I am *always* respectable. If anyone chooses not to respect me, however…" He gave his aunt a low grin. "There's very little I can do about that, is there?"

"Pish-tosh," Miss Walsh said. "I so hate when men are respectable. It usually involves rather too much posturing."

"Nonsense. You remember old Barnabas Tucker? Well, he…"

And they were off, as they so often were, on the sort of conversation that would have offended the more proper households three-quarters of a mile to the north.

"Speaking of Barnabas and his unfortunate predilections," Miss Walsh said, "have you all heard what happened at Redding Copy House?"

The other two women shook their heads and made little tsking noises.

"Badly run," Harriet said. "Staff constantly embezzling. No discretion in the clientele. I was certainly not surprised when it closed."

"I am so glad to not have to labor in my advanced age," Miss Walsh was saying. "It leaves me free to pursue leisure activities in my final years. Like—"

"Cheating us all at cards," Ree put in.

Yes. That was their favorite pastime of a winter evening: playing whist and cheating wildly. Cheating was the unspoken rule of the game. Cheating, in fact, was the *only* real rule of the game, and the competition was cutthroat.

Much of England would have summed up these three women with one word: whores. They'd won that epithet by virtue of the poverty they'd labored through, the men they'd associated with, and the color of their skin.

It wouldn't have mattered if they'd ever sold sexual services on the streets. They'd been poor. Aunt Ree and May Walsh were too dark to be considered anything other than unacceptably foreign; Harriet Cathing's mother had also been what the uptight middle class would call a whore.

They had never been seen as respectable by England's rules. The rules had written them out of the game centuries ago.

Crash set his bag down. "I've brought rum, milk, bread, spices, potatoes, and eggs. It's cold and you're almost out of everything."

Harriet beamed at him. "How utterly darling. He brings rum. Ree, I must get myself a nephew like him. How ever does one obtain one?"

Ree rolled her eyes. "Don't let the rum fool you. It's scant penance for all the woe he's brought into my life. Fortunately for us all, Crash is one of a kind."

Crash waggled his eyebrows at his aunt. "You know you love me."

She glowered at him. "Unfortunately."

"I've always meant to ask. What sort of a name is Crash? Is it a first or a family name?" Miss Walsh frowned at him. "That can't be your real name, can it?"

"His Christian name is Nigel," Ree put in, "but we started calling him Crash at a very young age, and it stuck so well that we've just decided to forget there was ever anything else. As for family names, we don't deal in those. It's a bit of a tradition. But if you feel better calling him Nigel—"

"Refer to me as Nigel again," Crash said with a raised finger, "and I'll start calling you Catriona."

His aunt made a face. "You don't want him," she explained earnestly to her friend. "He talks back. And he only brings enough rum for a little glass here and there. He's hardly worth all the bother."

But she gave him a proud smile.

And oh, he *had* been a bother. Never sitting still, always moving. Once, when he'd been a child scarcely old enough to learn his letters, he'd lived up to his assumed name. He'd dashed around a corner in a store and had run headlong into a display of canned goods. They'd toppled to the ground with a resounding crash.

The shopkeeper had grabbed him up, shaking him viciously, calling him a good-for-nothing hell-bent bastard who would end his days in a noose.

"Just like your father," he'd said. "But then, you don't even know who that is, do you, you worthless little mongrel?"

His aunt had taken Crash's hand and conducted him out of the shop.

"Don't you listen to him," she had said, her voice shaking. "He can't see you, not as you are. So don't you listen to what he says. You're good for anything you want to do. You'll have to try harder, and you'll have to do it a little differently—but don't you ever listen to him."

Twenty-six years of *don't you listen to him.*

Every time someone crossed the street at the sight of him. Every time someone spat in his direction. When the vicar announced at Sunday service that unnatural attractions to men were a sign of moral turpitude. The morning when a well-meaning woman had sought him out in a crowd and earnestly explained that foreign heathens like him needed to learn of Christ and seek divine forgiveness.

For twenty-six years, his aunt had told him not to listen to any of them. After all she'd done for him, a little rum was the least he could offer.

"You know," Miss Walsh put in, "if we could get this fine young man to play Martha's hand for us, nobody could use her to cheat."

Three faces considered this contemplatively. Crash was fairly certain that all three women were considering the many ways he might choose to play Martha's hand.

"Speak for yourself," Ree said piously. "I never cheat. I win by skill."

This was met with the raucous laughter it deserved.

Ha. She'd give up cheating the day she... No, he didn't want to think such morbid thoughts. His aunt was fifty-four; she had decades left in her, God willing. She'd taught him everything he knew about cheating. Cheating was the only way to win, and so she did it assiduously.

He sat and dealt.

"He won't do for a fourth," Harriet said. "But you know, May…"

May frowned. "I know. It's been a year. We should…consider a replacement now."

"I am not available on a permanent basis," Crash said smoothly. "My innocent young ears would burn off if I had to listen to more than an evening of your conversation."

They all laughed good-naturedly.

"Young man," said Miss Walsh, "you do realize that we know you?"

"Who?" he asked. "Me? You must be thinking of Nigel."

Ree had taught him to cheat, too, with everything he had in him. When the rules were stacked against you, cheating was a moral necessity.

A moment earlier in the day flashed in front of him— Daisy looking up at him in disapproval.

Stop flirting with me, she had said.

As if he *wanted* to flirt with her. Every time he saw her, every time she threw her so-perfect fiancé in his face, he became more and more certain that he'd had the luckiest of escapes. All those months spent worrying while he was in Paris…they'd been for nothing. He'd hoped for a letter. A telegram. A single word.

Not a damned thing had come. He'd not thought her the sort of person who would treat him like a shameful secret, one to be hidden as soon as possible. He was done flirting with Daisy.

She could have her emporium and her sweetheart. He'd learned long ago not to waste tears on anyone who pushed him away. Not shopkeepers. Not stablehands. Not even sweethearts he'd once intended to marry.

He smiled and poured little jiggers of rum for the women who had raised him. They had told him not to listen when the country shouted that he was nothing. They had taught him to walk with his head held high, to act as if he meant something even though nobody else would agree.

He wouldn't spare a thought for the woman who'd decided he meant nothing. He didn't want her back. He didn't care how she felt about him.

All he wanted was for Daisy Whitlaw to realize how wrong she'd been and to regret her stupidity. He wanted her to marry her stupid sub-lieutenant and have equally stupid children and look out her stupid window and think occasionally: *I suppose Crash was right after all. I made a mistake.*

Aside from that? He didn't care one bit. He wouldn't let himself do it.

Chapter 3

aisy was always going to feel like an interloper on her Sunday visits to her best friend. She'd resigned herself to that fact.

It didn't matter that Judith ushered her into a front salon as if she were regular company. The walls of the luxurious room were covered in a white-and-gold damask silk. The table Daisy sat at was laden with goodies: biscuits, sandwiches, scones.

Once, Judith had lived just across the street from Daisy. At first Daisy had felt she was the luckier of the two. Her father might have failed as a grocer, but he'd had a bit of an annuity, and her mother had been frugal enough, and genteel enough, to teach Daisy everything she had needed to know. Then Daisy's life had jagged down. Her father had died; his annuity had disappeared. Her mother had become ill. Alongside that, Judith's luck had jagged up, and then up again. She'd married a wealthy, powerful man she had known from her childhood. Now, instead of exchanging bread recipes and household tips, the two women sat at a table where three years of Daisy's labor would not pay for all the china.

"Here," Judith said with a smile. "Would you care for a roast beef sandwich?"

"Of course I would," Daisy said with a smile.

Once, Daisy and Judith had gone shopping together and joked of purchasing kid gloves with diamonds. They'd talked about adding gold leaf to their meager meals. It had been silly, ridiculous—and utterly necessary for Daisy's peace of mind. Their little game had provided perspective on her wants. *Your wishes are silly. Be happy you have soup bones, Daisy. You could have less.*

"How goes the flower shop?" Judith asked.

"It prospers." Daisy gave her friend as confident a smile as she could muster. "In fact, I've been awarded additional compensation for my valiant efforts. We're positively flush."

Not a lie. Five pence more a week—it had gone a long way. She and her mother were actually saving money in winter now, not bleeding it slowly away in coal bills.

Judith smiled, as Daisy had known she would.

The sad thing was, their friendship was already over. Judith just didn't know it yet. There was the literal distance between them—four miles, difficult for Daisy to manage on her own unless Judith sent a carriage, as she'd done today.

There was the way the maid's eyes cut toward Daisy as she placed the tea on the table, as if Daisy were a bit of refuse that she longed to sweep from the room. There was the fact that Daisy suspected Judith's servants earned more in a week than the owner of the flower shop bestowed on Daisy. Daisy would have been lucky to scrub floors for her friend.

"Tell me all the gossip," Judith said. "I don't want to miss a single story."

Daisy went through all their former mutual acquaintances: Fred Lotting and his wife, Mr. Padge, Daisy's mother… She talked of everyone but herself.

Daisy was lying to herself, she realized as they spoke and laughed. They *were* still friends. They still had those years of poverty binding them together. Judith had been her support, the shoulder she cried on when everything went wrong. In turn, she'd held her friend through every reversal.

They were friends still, fragile though that friendship was. Their hours together felt like spider silk—ready to dissipate with one good sweep of a servant's broom. One day it would break. One day. Still, it held. Spider webs tended to remain in place if you held your breath when you were close.

Daisy was trying not to breathe.

"Is there anything else?" Judith asked.

Daisy almost told Judith what she'd done about the charity bequest. She almost told her of entering the competition, of the grocer mocking her because she wasn't a man.

She didn't, though.

Daisy's Emporium was a dream that was as unattainable and unrealistic as gold leaf on radishes. Deep down, Daisy knew it would never come to pass. Dreaming was one thing. Entering a competition she couldn't win? That was a little worse.

Telling her friend about it? That would make this serious. *Real.* Judith would want to hear the details. She might even offer to help. And if she did…

Daisy would end up another one of Judith's servants, running a storefront for her. And if the store failed the way her father's store had…?

She did her best not to breathe on the attenuating cobwebs of their friendship.

"No," Daisy said instead. "That's all there is. All this about me, and we've scarcely spoken of you. How are you? How are the terrors?"

The terrors were Judith's younger brother and sister.

Judith laughed. "I'm well, as you can see." She gestured around the room. "Theresa's being fitted for dresses at this very moment. Imagine her in silks, if you will."

Daisy couldn't imagine that sort of transformation. Judith's younger sister was a hellion at the best of times. She'd rip a silk gown in a minute flat. She'd smear grease on the skirts.

But of course, the cost of repair would no longer matter to her friend. And who knew how a deportment teacher might have changed the girl she remembered from a few months ago?

"We're well," Judith said. "Very well, and I'm glad to see you. I miss you. A few stolen hours here and there are hardly enough."

"I miss you, too." A few hours was all Daisy had. "But I need to go back to my mother."

"I know, dear." Judith patted her hand. "Is there anything you need?"

Daisy could have laughed. *Everything.* She needed everything.

"Gold leaf," she said instead. "Gold leaf and diamonds at my hem, and with that, I should be splendid."

Judith smiled at her.

It wouldn't be much longer until their friendship diminished to nothing. Until that moment, though, Daisy would let the servants frown at her. She wouldn't flinch when they kept too-careful an eye on her as they conducted her to the door, hoping to catch her in the act of stealing the silver.

Daisy took her leave, her smile plastered firmly on her face. She kept it there for three whole minutes before the reality of her life set in again.

She'd entered a competition she couldn't win. She'd agreed to let a man she didn't like assist her in her preparations.

Of course she hadn't told Judith. Judith knew she was poor; she didn't need to know that she'd gone witless.

rash was already late. Five minutes ago, the clock had chimed three. Daisy still found herself waiting in front of the general store. She was exhausted from her day at the flower shop, the wind was cold, and her patience was running thin.

Late was perhaps a little unfair. She knew he was around somewhere because his velocipede was leaning against the side of a building. But he was not present, and she'd not so much free time that she could afford to waste a moment of it.

Especially not if he had arrived on his velocipede. Just looking at the thing made her palms itch. She had done her best *not* to learn about the contraption when he'd first started riding it a few months back. She had been certain that he was going to live up to his name and crash into something.

That was because Crash on a velocipede belonged in a circus act, one that should have been paired with lions and flaming hoops. If she'd had any idea what a velocipede was when he first mentioned the thing, she would have protested. He'd called it a vehicle. Some vehicle it was; it couldn't even stand upright on its own. It was nothing but two wheels, one in front of the other. Nothing to stabilize it. No sticks to keep him upright.

Worse, Crash turned those wheels not by propelling himself with his feet on the ground. The wheels turned by means of little pedals attached to the front axle. A seat three or four feet above the ground might not seem so high, but he went flying past as fast as a horse could gallop.

She had to hide her face every time she saw him. She kept imagining him overbalancing. Or underbalancing. Or hitting a wall. She imagined him smashing into hard bricks at that speed…

She didn't care about Crash, not one bit. But just because he'd broken her heart didn't mean she wanted him to crack his skull.

Daisy was not the only one who had noted the velocipede's presence; three other women had observed it, and were standing—lollygagging, really—outside the store. Now, she could see him inside through the dirt-smeared windows. A cap covered his hair; he'd unwound his scarf so it was loosely looped around his neck, long enough to dangle enticingly just past his hips. He was gesturing, describing something to the store owner.

The storekeeper was laughing, ducking his bald head in amusement. Crash was *good* at making people laugh. He took nothing and nobody seriously, she reminded herself.

She wasn't the only one whose eyes drifted toward Crash's dim silhouette in the storefront. The other women ranged in age from sixteen-year-old Molly Jenkins, whose eyes glowed with the sort of unrequited worship that young girls needed to be warned about, to thirty-seven-year-old Martha Pratt, who really ought to have known better.

Daisy refused to join those three. They were doing their best to pretend they were just talking on the street corner. Talking, indeed. Talking out here in the cold, shifting from foot to foot and rubbing hands together, waiting, hoping that Crash would come out and warm them up.

Daisy had no such expectation. She'd already been burned.

She drifted a few yards down the pavement, letting her eyes stray to the pastries in the bakery window. Gingerbread men with iced pantaloons and colored buttons smiled vacantly onto the street. Cinnamon loaves, braided and laced with sugared nuts and sultanas, were laid in an enticing row. The air outside was laden with sweet and spice; she could almost taste that flaky crust. Buttery-looking scones flecked with bits of orange zest and currants made a mouth-watering pile.

It had been a very long time since breakfast.

Her stomach growled as the door to the general store opened behind her in a ring of bells. She wouldn't turn. She wouldn't look.

"Well, look who it is." She heard Miss Pratt speak. "It's Crash. What mischief are you up to today?"

"I've been looking for two items." Behind her, Crash's voice was low and velvety. "I procured the tinned ham. The carbolic smoke ball, however, was nowhere to be found."

These prosaic errands were met with a moment of disappointed silence.

"Oh." Miss Pratt let out a burst of laughter, as if nothing could be more amusing than oversalted pig meat in a metal container. "I *see*. Tinned ham *indeed.*"

Daisy wasn't going to turn around.

Young Miss Jenkins was not to be outdone. "Is this for your supper? Why, Crash, I've just realized. You don't even know who your people are. You must be very lonely. Aren't you positively *starved* for proper company?"

Crash laughed. "Someone has been feeding you poppycock. Who told you that? I can trace my lineage for generations."

"You can?" The girl was startled into momentary quiet.

It was a very short moment.

"That is to say, I had thought that…um…"

Daisy heard the rattle of metal. That was Crash taking his velocipede from the side of the building. "Don't spare

a moment of pity for me, Miss Jenkins," he said. "I come
from a long, illustrious line."

"You do?" That was Miss Pratt again, trying not to
sound dubious.

"I do." A note of infectious laughter touched his
voice. "I'm proud to say that I'm the scion of three
generations of dock whores and sailors."

He was so utterly impossible. Daisy choked into her
handkerchief and couldn't help looking behind her. Crash
was standing, his hand outstretched as if he were
declaiming some kind of poem. Only Crash could say he
was descended from prostitutes with that flair, as if it were
a thing to be delighted about. Only Crash could carry the
thing off so perfectly, smiling beatifically. He acted as if
everyone whose birth had been legitimized by something
as prosaic as marriage was somehow less fortunate than he.

Crash looked as if he'd never had horse dung thrown
at him. As if nobody had ever told him to behave in a
manner comporting with his station. As if he'd never
harbored doubts, as if he expected at any moment to be
informed that he'd been made mayor of all London. She
felt a brief tickle of jealousy that he should be so free of all
the rules that bound her. Daisy turned back to the bread
again.

She could scarcely pretend those fine, sugared
confections held her interest.

"Oh," Miss Jenkins managed in a strangled voice.

"Really," Crash said, "do you think I'd want a carbolic
smoke ball for myself? I'm young and in excellent health.
It's for my aunt. She's a little older, and with winter coming
on, I don't want her to take sick."

"Oh." That syllable was also a little strangled. "I'm
sorry to have asked."

"Don't be," Crash said cheerfully. "I daresay my
family is more interesting than yours. I merely wanted to

inform you that there's no need to squander your pity on me. I surely don't need it."

If Crash could bottle his arrogance and sell it to the masses, English society would crumble within a decade. They'd never be able to govern their empire, not with talk of ruling by right of blood. The peers of the realm would renounce everything, mount their velocipedes, and ride into the ocean en masse while he looked on and laughed.

"But... Don't you ever wish for...for..."

"What?" Crash said. "Are you asking if I ever hope that maybe one day, a lovely young lady of good breeding and decent education might take pity on me, and I might give up all my wicked ways? Do you think that maybe I yearn for someone to transform me? Someone who will turn me from my path of sin with one speaking look?"

None of the women answered. Daisy imagined they were all silent, caught in the thralls of lust. He must know she was listening.

"Wonder no more," Crash said. "I'm just looking for someone to share my..."

He paused, and the women sighed.

"What?" whispered Molly.

"My potted meat," Crash said, exaggerating the word *meat* so there was little doubt that he was referring to something other than ham in tins. "What else?"

She couldn't bear it any longer. Daisy turned to him. "Crash, stop tormenting those poor souls. You're like a cat with a butterfly—you never can stop playing."

"Allow me to defend myself, Miss Whitlaw." Crash winked at her. "I wasn't tormenting them. I was tormenting *you*. Did I do a proper job of it?"

"You don't do proper jobs." She sniffed. "*That* was always the problem."

Crash inclined his head, as if granting her that point. "Ladies. I must be off." He held his velocipede by the handles and walked toward her. "Come, Daisy. We've much to discuss."

She shouldn't have agreed to this. She shouldn't have come here. As he stalked toward her, her stomach turned. Oh, she wished it were nausea.

She folded her hands. "We do," she said. "Let's start with this. You should have been more punctual."

Crash folded his arms. "I've spent the day looking for a space for my shop. There's little available, none of it in the right location. Find the right location, and the space is wrong. One place was perfect, but twice as large as I need." He glowered in her direction, as if this were her fault. "On top of all that, I've been trying to obtain a carbolic smoke ball. So yes, Daisy, I do apologize. My future and my aunt's continued health should have taken second place to your minor discomfort."

"Thank you. I take your apology for precisely what it is worth." Daisy knew how she ranked in his estimation. "Your shop? What are you selling?"

He didn't look at her. "You remember. I'm not in the mood to pretend otherwise."

So he still intended to sell his damned velocipedes. Idiot plan. Only a fool would want them.

He was probably going to make a fortune. There were always idiots out there willing to pay money to kill themselves. Crash had never had any problem obtaining *his* wishes.

A little steering column was attached to the front wheel of his velocipede. He took hold of this and began guiding the contraption down the street, walking next to her. Thank God he wasn't riding. She'd have had to crane her neck to look at him, and she felt uncomfortable enough in his presence.

It had been one of those days. She had been up since four that morning, tying bouquets.

He didn't say anything. He didn't tell her where they were headed or what he had planned. The wheels of his velocipede made a curious staccato sound as they passed over the cobblestones.

Crash's silence had once been welcoming, for lack of a better word. He had kept silent the same way another man might stand up from a seat on an omnibus. It used to make her feel as if he were making room for her.

This quiet felt disapproving.

"Oh, shut up, Crash," she said, even though he hadn't said anything at all. "I'm sure you had a jolly day making wagers on my eventual public embarrassment and searching for your…balls."

He made a little choking sound. "My carbolic smoke ball, you mean?"

"I spent *my* day at honest labor." Her voice shook. "Honest labor where every man who found me alone felt it was his right to pinch my behind."

"So why is getting your behind considered honest labor, while—" He cut himself off. "Never mind. I'm not arguing with you." He glanced at her and shook his head. "Walk faster. We're almost there."

She trotted after him. They turned a corner and traversed a street. He dragged his velocipede through the mud of a park before he turned to look at her.

"Where are we going?" she asked.

He gestured to an abandoned gravel footpath that followed the line of a canal. The waters were brown and stagnant, running sullenly through the gray warehouses on either side. "Here."

"Here?" She chafed her hands together. "What are we doing *here?* Could we not go somewhere warmer?"

"No." He gave her a not-quite-friendly smile. "We can't. You see, I'm going to teach you how to ride my velocipede."

For a second, she had an image of herself hurtling into the canal at full speed. She flinched back. "Oh no. No. There isn't a chance of it. That is not at all what I had in mind."

He pushed the contraption toward her. "Oh, yes," he countered. "You are going to learn."

She shook her head more violently. "First, your stupid veloci-whatever has nothing to do with the competition. Second, I could not walk on a fence rail without falling off, ever. I have no balance to speak of, let alone enough to manage that—thing. I'm not here to ride your da—your dratted veloci…tastrophe. You said you were going to help me win."

"I did," he said. "And this is how you're going to do it. You're going to—"

"Let me guess: I'm going to wear a revealing outfit, come flying through the crowd on a velociclysm, hurtle through a flaming hoop, and land on the stage to tumultuous applause."

He blinked and looked at her. "Well, that would be *one* way to manage it. But I had quite a different idea in mind. See, there's a trick to riding a velocipede."

"You have to be a lunatic." Daisy sniffed.

"Correct," Crash said. "You have to be a lunatic, although that is rather unkind to the lunatics, don't you think?"

She made a noise in her throat in response.

"Here's the trick: you have to not care. Our bodies learn motion from walking. When you're walking, you learn to balance on your feet, to stay upright as you move. Height frightens us; speed more so. But all the rules we've told ourselves must be true about motion in general? They're wrong when we're on a velocipede."

He was warming to his subject matter. He leaned the contraption against a bench and began to use his hands to demonstrate.

"On a velocipede," he told her, "you don't need to balance."

"How do you stay upright?"

"The faster you go, the more stable you are."

She snorted in disbelief.

"I know it sounds unlikely, but it's true. When you turn, you might be afraid that you'll fall. You won't—but to make sure, you should lean into the direction you're turning."

"Poppycock." She swallowed. "You're trying to get your revenge. You're trying to kill me."

He gave her an unreadable look. "You never did believe me, Daisy. No matter what you think of the other times we disagreed, *this* time I am simply right. The velocipede is a simple application of the principles of natural law. You've spent your entire life learning lessons. *Stupid* lessons. Keep quiet if a man pinches your bum. Don't speak loudly, or you'll turn heads. Express yourself in the mildest possible terms, so that no one can have any objection. There are reasons you have to act that way on a daily basis. But if you want one damned chance at success at this competition you've entered, you're going to have to forget them all. You can't forget *some* rules and hope for the best."

She swallowed. She looked at the machine leaning peacefully against the bench. "But I could *die.*"

He didn't call her overly dramatic. He didn't roll his eyes.

Instead, he raised an eyebrow. "Daisy," he said slowly, "I assume you entered the competition to establish yourself. Because you wanted lasting financial security. At present, your future rests entirely on other people continuing to provide you with gainful employment. What do you think would happen if that stopped?"

He didn't need to ask her to imagine what would happen if she had no money. If she were tossed from her rooms, if she couldn't afford bread, if her mother…

Daisy didn't want to think of her mother. She swallowed. "I'm…I'm not going to win."

"Ah, ah." He held up a finger. "None of that. My only point is that there's no way around risk." He gestured her forward. "That is precisely why you're learning to ride a velocipede. If you're going to risk your life, you had best risk it properly."

She frowned. She was fairly certain there was a flaw in his logic. He'd always been able to convince her of anything and everything. Wagers? They were harmless, so long as nobody bet money they couldn't afford to lose. His prior liaisons with men and women? Well, so long as he was honest about what happened, and hadn't lied to anyone, who was hurt by it? She'd been so turned around that she'd accepted it all. Even now, she was certain that he had been wrong. She just wasn't sure how.

"One more thing." His eyes met hers. "It's called a *velocipede*. Or a bicycle. You're not stupid, so use its proper name. Call the product I will be selling a *velocitastrophe* one more time, and I will…"

They watched each other for a long moment.

"You'll what?" she asked. "Push me over?"

His lip curled in distaste. "I'll make polite conversation. Like this: How is your fiancé, Daisy? When did you last hear about him? Was his last letter everything you hoped for?"

His eyes were dark and narrowed, looking down at her, and Daisy felt a little shiver slide up her spine.

She swallowed. It was an excellent threat. "Him?" She hadn't even given him a name. "Why would that bother me? I would gladly talk about…Edwin."

"I'm sure you would. He sounds like quite the stick-in-the-mud. The two of you no doubt get along splendidly."

Chapter 4

For a second, Crash thought Daisy would turn away. Instead, her chin went up. Her fingers, clothed in dark gray wool gloves, clenched at her side. Her eyes glittered like shards of blue glass.

"Go ahead," she said. "I'm not afraid of you or your threats or your velossacre."

"Velossacre?"

"I'm making this up as I go along." She glowered at him defiantly. "It's derived from massacre. If you kill me with that thing, at least you'll hang for my death. I take what scant satisfaction I can find in this cruel world."

Damn it all. He didn't want to remember why he'd once liked her.

He simply tsked instead. "Daisy, you know that my slightly less-than-legal activities are chosen so as not to harm anyone. I'm a reprobate, not a villain. Veloci-probate hasn't the same ring."

Her nose wrinkled. "No. That sounds like an exceedingly swift Court of Chancery."

"Ugh. Nobody wants that."

She almost smiled. Almost. "Very well. How does one even get on this…monstrosipede?"

He wasn't going to take the bait. Instead, he guided her to a bench, one where she could hop up and reach the seat of his velocipede. It was a simple matter to brace the machine against his hip and gesture her forward.

"So," he said. "Get on."

"What, with you holding it?"

"Yes." He rolled his eyes. "With me holding it. Do you think I'm going to let you fall?"

She gave him a dark look. Her nose twitched. "You might."

"I might," he said, returning her dark look. "That's one of the risks you'll have to take."

She glared at him for a long moment before gathering her skirts to the ankles, awkwardly straddling the metal top bar, and lowering herself gingerly to the seat.

She shut her eyes instantly, clutching the handlebar. "Oh, God. It's very high. And *extremely* wobbly."

"Well, then," Crash said sarcastically. "I suppose our lesson is done. We'll leave the having of trades to men, and you can keep on getting your bum pinched in your flower shop."

Her eyes flew open.

"That's better," he said. "Yes. It's high and wobbly. That's because you're not moving. Now I'm going to come around to the side, and you're going to put your feet on the pedals. Understand?"

"But…"

He moved without waiting, and she winced as the machine lurched beneath her.

"You're touching me," she said as his hand landed against her spine. "I said, no—"

He pulled his hands away and held them up in the air. The velocipede faltered, tilted, and—

"Touch me!" she shrieked. "I lied! I don't mind!"

He calmly took hold of her before she fell. "Come now, Daisy. I'm not touching you for my pleasure. If you die, I hang, and hanging is not in my plan. Besides, you have a sweetheart. I won't do anything that your dear Edwin won't approve of. My promise."

She gave him a baleful glare.

"So," he said. "Feet on the pedals. Push first on the top one. No, not to the side—down, smoothly down. Like that. Now the next."

It took her a few revolutions to get the gist of the motion. She went slowly; he paced beside her. They started along the canal at a snail's pace. He kept one hand on the seat, the other on her spine, steadying her as she moved.

"A little faster," he told her. "I can keep up."

A little faster meant there was a bit of wind as they moved. The breeze whipped her bonnet off her head and left it trailing behind her, held in place only by bonnet strings. It stole little tendrils of pale hair from Daisy's braid. A little faster meant that his hand was no longer steady against her spine. His palm jogged with his pace, up and down, up and down.

The cold lent color to her cheeks. Her determination gave fire to her eyes. God, he missed Daisy.

It wasn't the first time he had missed her.

It happened at odd intervals. When he heard an amusing story and thought of telling her. When he had an idea he wanted to share with her. When he saw her on the street and accidentally smiled before he remembered.

He didn't *really* miss her. He missed the woman he'd once believed she was.

But he missed that woman now, almost intensely. He missed the way she gritted her teeth as she concentrated. He missed the way she kept trying, no matter what life threw at her. The way she gripped the handlebar, as if holding on more tightly would save her from a fall.

He missed the way she'd once trusted him, the way she had used to look at him.

"See?" he told her through even breaths as he ran alongside her. "Keep going. You're still very high up, but you're less wobbly, aren't you?"

Her teeth gritted. "Maybe."

"You can go faster."

"But if I do?"

"I'll be right here," he lied.

She went faster.

It wasn't hard to get to the point where he couldn't keep pace with her on the velocipede. She had her gaze trained ahead; she didn't even notice when it happened. He let go and she kept on pedaling. For one moment, then two. Her grip relaxed. Her teeth stopped gritting together.

Her expression began to soften into exhilarating wonder.

It lasted for precisely one second. Then she realized that he was no longer supporting her. She looked around, jerked the handlebar—

Crash winced as she toppled to the ground. He jogged up to where she lay on the path, a tangle of skirts and pedals and indignation.

She pushed herself up on her hands, brushing gravel away. "You said you'd hold me up!"

"I lied," he said succinctly.

She unraveled her scarf from the mess on the ground and unwound her skirts from the pedal where they'd tangled. "I ought to have known."

"It was worth it," he said. "You had the feel of the velocipede for one second. For one second, you understood. All you have to do is go fast enough, and you don't wobble. You fell because you *stopped*. Not because of me. That's how it works. Don't stop. Don't question. Go faster."

She brushed debris from her skirts and stood. "What has any of this to do with Daisy's Emporium?"

"You let fear stop you," he told her. "You stood up in front of the crowd and lost your nerve. I know you, Daisy." And he did, a little. "Your figures are no doubt sound. Your plan is well thought out. You've likely researched every last item you want to sell in your shop. You know how much you can purchase it for in quantity and how much it will sell for. None of that matters, because nobody will ever know how good you are if you lose your nerve. That's what you need to work on, Daisy. Not your speech, not your facts. Your nerve. You will be high up in front of everyone with no support, and when you get scared, you can't falter. You need to go faster."

"You…" Her jaw squared and she looked at him with suspicious eyes. "You think my plan is well thought out?"

"I'm not going to repeat myself."

One of the things he'd once loved about Daisy was this. She looked down at her skirts, now decorated with a liberal smear of muddy snow down the side. She shook gravel from her gloves. Her jaw squared and she lifted her chin.

"Very well. I'm getting back on."

It took Daisy an hour to achieve the minimum skill she needed to pedal down the footpath. An hour of wobbling and catching herself. An hour during which she fell twice. Her gloves tore. Her gown ripped. Daisy gritted her teeth and kept going.

An hour of Crash watching her, his heart aching for what they had almost been to each other. It was an hour until he steadied the velocipede against the bench one final time. Until he took her hand to keep her from falling as she dismounted and almost didn't want to let go.

"Tomorrow?" he asked. "You need more practice."

She shook her head. "The next day. I need… I need…" She didn't say what she needed. She stood on the bench she'd used to disembark and looked down at him with wide, hurt eyes.

"Why?" she asked finally. "Why are you really doing this?"

Of course she knew it wasn't about the damned wagers. If she'd talked to anyone at all about him, she had to know he'd refused to take any bets about the charity bequest at all.

"Because." His voice came out a growl. "Because I want you to understand for once. I don't get to stand still—if I do, I will fall. Unlike you, I never had a choice. If I start to wobble, I have to go faster."

She flinched. "I *said* I was sorry."

"I recall that you said you forgave me." At length. That unwished-for absolution still rankled.

"And that's why you're still angry? I've seen you brush off harsher insults a thousand times."

He held up a hand. "No. That's where and why this ends. Tell yourself I could have lived differently all you wish. I can't stop you; you are remarkably good at lying to yourself."

She stared at him.

"I am *good* at going fast," Crash said. "So good that sometimes all anyone sees is a blur. Insult me all you like. Deep down, though, you know better. You know who I am."

Her eyes glittered back at him. "I know you very well, Crash. *Everyone* knows. You make a point of it."

The things everyone knew about him… He held up a hand. "No. That's where and how this ends. Tell yourself I could have lived differently all you wish. I can't stop you; you are remarkably good at lying to yourself."

She stared at him.

His teeth ground together. "But don't lie about me when I'm standing right here. I don't need your holy dispensation to exist."

"Just as well," Daisy shot back. "You don't have it."

Daisy unwound her scarf and set her ruined gloves in a wad on the entry table. Her body ached from the exertion and from the falls. She'd be sore the next day.

How fitting. Crash had a tendency to leave her sore in the morning.

The single room that she shared with her mother was still warm, a good sign. She always had to tell her mother to burn coal and never mind the cost. Winter was hard on her, and heat was one of the few things that kept her mother's pains away.

Today, her mother had actually listened.

"Mother?" Their flat was a scant two rooms—one, really, but they'd rigged a curtain. Somehow, two tiny rooms seemed more luxurious than one small one. She peered around the fabric into the alcove where their shared bed stood. "Mother?"

She could smell something delicious—crisp jacket potatoes and something savory that might have been fish. But there was no answer.

Good. Her mother wasn't here. Daisy found a rag and scrubbed at the mud on her skirt. The hem needed repairing, but it could be fixed. For now, a pin or two would manage.

She'd hastily tacked the fabric in place when the door opened behind her. Daisy turned guiltily. "Oh, Mama. There you are."

Her mother removed her own scarf and gave Daisy a bright smile. "I'm feeling better today. I was thinking that perhaps I'd take on a little more lacework instead of just the two pieces a week we agreed upon."

It was always a delicate balance. The more her mother earned, the easier it was to purchase coal. The more her mother worked, the worse her rheumatism became.

"Mama." Daisy stood and set her hand on her mother's shoulder. "The last time you tried, your rheumatism had you laid up for weeks. It's not worth it."

Rheumatism. That's what they assumed it was. Years ago, they had spent money they didn't have for a physician. When he'd come, he'd examined her mother for a cursory three minutes. Then he'd pulled Daisy aside.

"There is nothing wrong with your mother," he had told her in a quiet voice. "Women of her age don't get rheumatism. She is malingering. She wishes to stay in bed, and so she's invented aches and pains to do so. She doesn't need compassion or medical treatment. She needs someone to insist that she work."

Daisy had wanted to slap the man's supercilious expression off his face. Instead, she'd paid his fee. So much for physicians, then.

"I have supper ready," her mother said, "and I cleaned up a little—it does look nice, doesn't it?"

"It does."

"Sit," her mother said. "Eat."

They sat.

"Tell me about your day."

Daisy looked over at her mother. Her hair was beginning to go white in wisps. Daisy still thought her pretty. She had a lovely smile. But speak of unrealistic wishes. Here was one. A single woman could hardly support an aging mother on her own.

Daisy knew it. The doctor had known it. Her *mother* knew it. Her friends tried to hint at it, to tell Daisy that she should—gently—do her best to disentangle herself.

Daisy held on through sheer stubbornness. They would make do as long as Daisy had good work. As long as neither of them got sick. As long as nothing bad ever happened, she could manage it all.

She couldn't think of her mother, and her mother's future, without feeling a little ill.

She didn't want to talk about her day. She considered all her possible responses.

"I did some research," Daisy said instead.

"What sort of research?"

"Research into the sorts of new businesses that are opening shortly." Daisy frowned and speared a bite of potato.

"Oh? Anything interesting?"

Daisy considered the white lump on her fork. "There's a shop that is selling…um. Velocipedes."

"Whatever is a velocipede?"

"It's…" How to even describe the thing? "A metal frame. With wheels. Difficult to describe." She trailed off, mid-twirl of her fork, and looked at her mother's pursed lips.

"That's a thing that people would purchase? Why?"

Now that she'd ridden one, she could understand. There had been a moment of exhilaration. A sense that she could fly.

Daisy shrugged. "It's not much stupider than, say, a carbolic smoke ball."

"A *what?*"

"Another thing." She frowned. "For invalids. It's supposed to prevent influenza."

"Fools and their money." Her mother sighed. "Fools and their money. Drat it, why don't we know more fools?"

Daisy smiled. "I shall have to expand the circle of our acquaintance."

Her mother turned and contemplated Daisy. "You know, Daisy, it's probably time that you start looking for a fool."

Her heart sank. "You mean so that I can sell him a carbolic smoke ball?"

Her mother reached out and touched her hand. "To marry."

Daisy looked away. She felt raw. Unready for this conversation.

"Youth won't last forever," her mother said. Her fingers tightened on Daisy's hand. "I know you're telling yourself that you have time…"

Daisy's fingers lay quiescent under her mother's while her stomach churned. *You are remarkably good at lying to yourself.* Crash was wrong; she knew perfectly well how things were.

"You have to take care of yourself," her mother was saying. "Establish yourself. Have you seen a girl working in a flower shop above the age of thirty?"

Daisy shook her head.

"There's a reason for that." Her mother's grip tightened subtly on Daisy's hand. "It's like those flowers you sell. Nobody wants them after they've begun to wilt. I know I sound terribly mercenary, but Daisy, dear, you don't have to *love* him. You just have to be able to pretend well enough."

Here was the thing: Daisy wouldn't be marrying for herself, and her mother knew it. On her own, she might support herself indefinitely.

The person she could not support was her mother. Her emporium was a dream. No, worse; a distraction. It was a plaything she held up to pretend her future might be different than it was.

But this was the stark reality she faced. She needed to find a fool who wouldn't mind—or notice—her lack of virginity. If she didn't, one day she would have to walk away from the woman who had raised her because she could no longer afford her care.

It didn't matter how little Daisy wanted that to happen. It didn't matter how sick she felt at the thought. Coins didn't lie.

Daisy could only hope she hadn't ruined her chances at marriage. If she couldn't marry, if nobody ever wanted her…

She couldn't think of that.

She *had* to think of that.

Crash was right. Daisy was remarkably good at lying to herself. One day, she'd stop hoping to come to her own rescue. One day, she'd recognize that there was no escape. She'd do her best to find herself a fool of a fiancé, because she knew she wouldn't leave her mother. She couldn't.

When that happened, when she smiled at some man with half her sense, Crash would think the worst of her. He'd call her a liar and a cheat and more. He wouldn't be wrong.

There were some things one could not say to one's mother.

I cannot marry yet. There's this man I hate—incidentally, the one who took my virginity—and he would poke fun at me.

No, it was time to grow up and face the truth. She couldn't care what Crash would say.

She smiled at her mother instead. "I know." Her cheeks hurt, holding that false expression.

Today was Monday evening. On Saturday, the judges would award the bequest to someone else. They would crush her dream. They'd make it clear that she'd told herself lies. At that point, she would have to accept what she had to do. She would *have* to stop hoping for an escape.

It was as inevitable as her mother's rheumatism.

"Sunday," Daisy said. "This Sunday. That's when I'll start looking."

Chapter 5

Daisy was glad for work early the next morning, even though she woke with every muscle in her body shrieking in protest at their ill-usage the day before. Work gave her an excuse to wash quickly and hide the bruise on her hip before her mother noticed. Work allowed her to leave before the sun rose.

She didn't have to think of her presentation or what would come after she lost. She arrived at the shop in the early morning hours and lost herself in her work, bunching together little bouquets of forced violets and tying them with ribbon. It was quiet work, comforting work; she didn't have to talk to anyone while she was doing it. She could just match flowers together and tie them with cord. White and purple; pink and lilac. Each little bouquet was a bit of happiness that she put together for someone else.

Today, though, she couldn't entirely lose herself in the activity. Her mother's words came back to her.

It's like those flowers you sell. Nobody wants them after they've begun to wilt.

Bouquets of temporary happiness. Purchased for a penny; discarded the moment they became inconvenient.

She could almost imagine Crash leaning close to her and whispering in her ear. *You are remarkably good at lying to yourself.*

She shoved her mental image of him away.

At least she enjoyed her work. She made people happy. She made them smile.

The shop bell rang and a woman peered in. She was wearing a sober working-woman's skirt of dark wool and a dingy gray shirtwaist—likely once white—with ink stains on the cuff.

Daisy summed the woman up with a single glance. She was likely one of the unmarried women who labored in the backroom of one of the nearby shops. Daisy had talked to many such women. She probably lived in a rooming house with dozens of other women. She saved her coins, one by one, dreaming of another life, a better life.

It would never come. Women never worked their way up. They started their life near their pinnacle and had only to fall from there.

Daisy had been instructed to shoo women like this away when she first started.

"They're trying to poach our heat," Mr. Trigard, the owner of the shop had grumbled. "They know we must warm the place for our flowers, and they're looking for a handout. They'll never purchase a thing."

For the first month, Daisy had done as Mr. Trigard said. Then he'd started trusting her, and he'd stopped coming in.

It turned out that inhospitality was not one of her talents. She'd given up and started making them bouquets in her spare moments. Not the exquisitely put-together sprays of baby's breath and rosebuds that she constructed for the gentility. Instead, she made little things, pretty things, with leftover bits: flowers cut too short, extra sprigs of leaves, scraps of ribbon that would otherwise have been discarded.

Her creations could be purchased for a halfpenny.

The woman looked from bucket to bucket, her lips pursed.

That was the thing about working in a flower shop. One learned to assess customers. A maid in crisp, brown livery buying for an entire household didn't want to dilly-dally over her purchase. She wanted Daisy to tell her what was available right away.

A woman who wandered in, glancing about timidly, was exactly the opposite. If Daisy launched herself in her direction the instant she entered the room, she'd disclaim all interest and slink away.

Give a customer a little time to start imagining a flower in her life, though, and she'd take it.

The woman stopped at the violets in a little metal tray filled with water, brushing the velvety green leaves with a single finger, before biting her lip and moving on.

It was November; the wares were much denuded. But then again, it was November, and so was the world. A single forced tulip could bring color to any room these days.

Daisy concentrated on tying ribbons and watched her customer beneath her lashes. The woman removed knit gloves carefully. She glanced at the hothouse rosebuds, looked at the golden lilies with wonder in her eyes, and then gave her head a little shake.

Time now for Daisy to intervene.

"Are you looking for a buttonhole or a bouquet?" she asked cheerily.

The woman jumped. "Oh. I hadn't thought."

Daisy pointed to her own buttonhole—a bright pink dahlia, smaller than usual, just over her right breast.

"Me personally, I prefer a buttonhole. They're not so expensive as a bouquet, but I can carry one around with me all day. That way I always have a little beauty close by."

The woman looked away. "Pardon me for saying so, but it seems extravagant. Flowers are for…" She gestured outside, at the rest of London. "Not really for someone like me."

Someone like *her*.

Maybe it was her conversation with her mother, but Daisy felt a kinship with the woman. This was who she would be in ten years if she didn't marry. Alone. Cloistered in a backroom, thinking that a halfpenny expenditure was too extravagant.

"Nonsense," Daisy said a little too sharply. "Whoever said that flowers aren't for you?"

The woman blinked.

Daisy knew the answer to that question. *Everyone* said that flowers weren't for her. The woman wasn't married and likely wasn't going to be. She worked for a living. She didn't have servants. She was supposed to be satisfied living a drab little life, just because everyone thought she was a drab little woman.

Drab women didn't get flowers. They didn't deserve beauty.

The woman glanced down. "It's such a luxury. I don't see…"

She had stopped in front of the yellow flowers. Daisy reached out and picked out a creation she'd made of a forced tulip that had snapped off its stem—nothing more than the brilliant yellow bud and a spray of green leaves.

"Here," Daisy said, holding it out. "It's a halfpenny. Tell me, Miss…" She trailed off.

The woman inhaled. "It's missus, actually." Her eyes shut. "Mrs. Wilde. My Jonas passed away five years ago, and…"

"Mrs. Wilde," Daisy said softly, "is there anyone who believes you're worth a halfpenny of beauty any longer?"

The woman shook her head.

"Well, then." Daisy gave her a nod. "Maybe the person who needs to believe it is you."

Daisy had done this before, convincing a reluctant woman to bring a little beauty into her life. She'd never felt guilty about it—but now she did. She could almost imagine Crash standing behind her, whispering in her ear.

My, you are *good at lying to yourself. Listen to you.*

She wasn't lying to herself. She wasn't. She *did* bring a little beauty into these women's lives; if she didn't, why did they all come back? Why would they bring their friends?

"I shouldn't." But Mrs. Wilde hadn't relinquished the tulip.

"Where do you work?"

Mrs. Wilde sighed. "The apothecary down the way. I weigh and measure for him and track his receipts." Her mouth pinched. "I keep track of whatever fine remedy is in vogue, make sure it's ordered and on the shelves. This month, it's the carbolic smoke ball."

Those damned carbolic smoke balls again.

"So you help hundreds of people take their medicine and get well," Daisy said.

"That's…one way of looking at it."

"I'd never tell you to spend money you don't have," Daisy said sympathetically. "But if you're saying you don't *deserve* this, with all that you do…?"

She let her words hang.

Mrs. Wilde looked at the tulip. She glanced down at her hands, out the door, and then back to the tulip. Then she gave a fierce little nod.

"Here." She opened her purse and removed a coin. "Take it before I change my mind."

It was worth it for the smile she saw on Mrs. Wilde's face as she left the shop. Daisy *was* selling happiness. Temporary happiness, very likely, but was there any other kind? Poor women deserved flowers as much as rich ones—more so, in fact. They had that much less beauty in their lives.

Daisy went back to making bouquets, but bouquet-tying was delicate work, and her fingers jerked the twine a bit too hard. She wasn't lying to herself, and she hadn't lied to Mrs. Wilde. She *hadn't*. Rich women were taught that their every wish would be granted. Women like Daisy? Like Mrs. Wilde? They were allowed nothing. They weren't even supposed to properly wish, not for anything worth having. They were allowed to subsist, and then only if they were lucky and useful.

Daisy wasn't lying to herself. She was just making it possible to get through one day and then the next, to find the little moments that made it possible to not dread her future.

That future loomed closer than ever.

Sunday. She'd promised her mother to start encouraging gentleman on Sunday. The very idea left her cold. No wonder she was wasting time submitting applications for a charity bequest. She wanted to believe she had a chance to get away.

She wasn't that naïve.

Daisy stared at her violets. They were just as pretty and just as purple as they'd been a few moments before.

"I don't lie to myself," she told them. "I know the truth all too well."

They looked up at her. Purple petals faded to white in the center, with a dot of yellow. Flowers couldn't really *look*. They didn't have eyes. So why did this batch seem to glower at her in disapproval?

She switched from making bouquets of violets to working with tulips. Putting a good face on things wasn't lying. She told herself the truth with scrupulous regularity. She was running out of time.

Running out of time to establish herself, running out of time to save her mother, running out of time to be anything except another drab woman in a drab occupation telling herself she didn't deserve so much as a halfpenny flower.

So she took a moment to make sure her dreams were well and thoroughly crushed before accepting the inevitable. What of it? Crash was wrong. She didn't *lie* to herself.

But then Crash had said that she'd lied about *him*. That was what rankled. She'd thought of that moment when everything had gone wrong between them over and over.

It had been after…after…

No, if she wasn't lying to herself, she could use the proper words.

It was after they had sex.

Speaking of stupidity. What sort of idiot was Daisy? He'd told her he needed to leave town. He'd said he would be gone to the continent for months. She'd thrown herself at him.

She was a first-class fool, and her face burned in memory.

But he'd been sweet, and it had been lovely, and… And then it had been over. They'd been in bed together, holding each other. She'd been naked and vulnerable and too much in love to realize she ought to have been scared.

"You know, Daisy," he had said. "I told you, you shouldn't have a thing to do with me. Look here. I've corrupted you." He'd kissed her.

"You never told me any such thing. Not seriously."

"True."

She'd kissed him back. "I don't mind being corrupted, if it's by you."

Now, she could flinch at her gullibility. Then, she'd leaned into him with complete trust.

He had sat up in bed. "I haven't explained to you why I'll be gone yet. I've a plan to turn…well, not respectable.

But." He had shrugged. "Something like. I've taken risks, but I can't keep doing that, not with a wife and a family."

Her heart had thumped wildly at those words. *Wife. Family.*

"I need to go to France," he told her. "There's a craze building there for velocipedes."

"What are those?"

"They're metal vehicles. With foot-pedals."

"With what?"

"One pushes the pedal with one's foot, and it turns a wheel…" He'd gone on.

It turned out there was no way to describe a velocipede, not with any number of words. She'd stared in confusion.

"It will all make sense when you see one." He'd given her a cocky grin. "They're on the verge of becoming a phenomenon in France. Give it five years, and they'll be the rage here, too. I'm going to have the premiere velocipede shop in all of London. But I'll need to visit factories, learn how to repair them… I'll be gone a while. Months, at least."

Her hands entwined with his.

"The way I see it," he said, "you could marry me and come with me."

She had inhaled.

"Or we could wait two months for me to go in order to be certain that nothing comes of what we just did. I would return to you as soon as I could."

That dose of reality had made Daisy stop and think.

"Crash." Daisy had leaned her head against his shoulder. "I can't leave my mother for months on end, and I can't see her traveling to France."

He'd kissed her. "Wait two months it is, then. That is, assuming you'll marry me despite my terribly checkered past. Will you?"

In the time since that night, Daisy had examined her response over and over.

"That depends," she had said teasingly. "Precisely how many checks does your past have?"

"Maybe one or two." His eyes had glinted wickedly.

"You can't fool me." She'd leaned in and kissed him. "There must be dozens. I know about the gambling."

"That? That's not really a check at all—just illegal." He had given her a cocky smile.

Daisy had heard this from him a great deal in the past months. In some ways, it had felt like Crash had suspended her good sense.

She'd started arguing his side to herself.

Who do I hurt if I kiss him? If I let him put his hand there? It can't really be wrong, not if it feels so right.

She'd told herself that so often that she'd almost completely believed it. Almost. She was already making excuses for him.

That had brought her to this moment, naked in bed with him.

"Really," he mused, "the only true check in my past was the time Jeremy and I robbed Mr. Wintour. But he deserved it, and everyone does stupid things when they're young…"

All Daisy's explanations had failed her at that moment. Her stomach had roiled uneasily, and the *almost* she could not quite dispel returned with a vengeance.

"You did what?"

"Oh, did I not tell you about that?" He'd given her a brilliant, unashamed smile. "Actually, it's an amusing story. Mr. Wintour, see, was Jeremy's employer at the time—you recall Jeremy, yes? In any event, he accused Jeremy of thievery. Which was…" Crash had shaken his head. "Stupid and wrong, and in any event, Jeremy was sacked without his wages. Taking matters into our own hands was a matter of justice…"

Daisy had scarcely heard the account that followed.

Who does it hurt? He had always asked her that question. He'd given her his magical smile, and she'd gone along. His magic had finally failed.

Who does it hurt?

Here, there was an answer. Never mind his earnest confession. Never mind that it wasn't that much or that Mr. Wintour had deserved it. Crash could only alter Daisy's sense of right and wrong so far, and stealing was wrong. Under all circumstances. It was wrong, demonstrably wrong.

Maybe he'd been wrong about everything else.

"It was nine years ago," he finished. "I was seventeen and stupid, and, well…"

And he was sorry now. She clutched at that. It had just been the once. Boys did stupid things.

Her thoughts might have been rationalizations, but she held tight to them. She had reached out and taken his hand impulsively.

"It doesn't matter," she had said. "I love you. I forgive you."

He'd frowned down at her fingers twining with his.

"You forgive me," he had finally said in a low tone. "Why do *you* forgive me? I didn't steal from you. What are you forgiving me for?"

"For everything," she had said earnestly. "I forgive you for *everything* you've done."

"Everything." The pleased animation had slipped from his face. The next words came slowly. "You forgive me for *everything*. Not just the one-time theft. Pardon me; I should like to have your *everything* spelled out."

She'd felt confused.

He pulled his arm from her. "Do you forgive me for taking wagers?"

"Of course."

"You forgive me my former lovers, I assume."

"Naturally."

Instead of appeasing him, each answer of hers made his face even more dangerous. "You forgive me for being a bastard, I suppose."

"You know I do."

His voice was low and cutting. "Next, you'll forgive me my aunt and my mother. You'll forgive me for not having English features, for the color of my skin, for—"

In the months since, she'd come to understand that she'd misstepped. She had said the wrong thing, precisely the wrong thing.

At the time, she'd thought she was reassuring him.

"Yes," she had said desperately. "I do. All of it."

"Then you surely *forgive* me for having the stones to believe I'm worth something."

She'd stared at him in confusion. "How can you doubt it?

He had pulled away from her, standing up, hunting in their clothing piled together for his trousers. "Very well. Do you want me to forgive you for your mother? *She'll* be a burden, that's for sure. Shall I forgive you for working in a shop? I know you flirt with the men who come by."

"Only a little—it doesn't mean anything, just enough to puff up their esteem—"

"Don't worry." He made the next words sound ugly. "I forgive you." His voice dropped. "I forgive you the fact that you were raised to think yourself better than you are."

She had gasped.

"I forgive you your impertinent and unwomanly desire to be more."

She had been beyond gasping.

"I forgive you your utter ignorance in bed," he had continued, "and your maidenly qualms. Hell, I'll forgive you your very existence in return. Even though, as these things are reckoned, you are a complete waste of a woman."

She felt as if she'd been flayed. As if she were as sore in her spirit as she'd been between her legs. She'd pulled the sheets about her.

"What are you saying?"

"What does it sound like I'm saying? I forgive you, Daisy. I forgive every miserable thing about you."

She had choked back tears, but his words hurt. Not because they were lies; they were all the truth. The truth she'd hoped he didn't see. The simple facts of her, laid bare.

She *was* ignorant about lovemaking. She *was* impertinent. Her mother *was* a burden.

"I'm only saying what you said," he told her. "I forgive you."

"Maybe I didn't say the right thing the right way." She'd struggled to understand. "But there's no call to hurt me like that. Good heavens, Crash, it's not like I wounded you."

Even now, even months later, it still hurt to remember his words. So she had said the wrong thing. What should it have mattered to him? She'd seen him shrug off worse insults, and her remarks had at least been kindly meant. His response… Now *that* had been truly unkind.

"Of course you didn't wound me," he had said. "I never feel pain. Why should I care if you do?"

She had been too devastated to think. "Get out." She'd scarcely managed those words.

"These are my rooms."

"I don't care." She turned away from him. "I can't look at you. I can't talk to you. Get *out.*"

He'd hesitated. Perhaps at that moment, he had realized that he'd said too much. "Daisy."

"Don't." If he talked to her, she would remember all the lies she told herself. She'd remember thirty minutes ago, when he had said he loved her, when he'd kissed her and entered her and talked to her and made her laugh. She'd remember that, instead of what he had just said.

"Daisy. Wait."

She had looked over at him. "For what?" she had said viciously. "For me to *forgive* you?"

He sat beside her. "I lost my temper. I have a— Oh, God, I have more than a little chip on my shoulder about some of this. And, well…" He had looked over at her. "I know everyone thinks I don't care. I can't let them know when I do. But I thought you understood me."

She had thought she had, too. "Did you mean it? Any of it, somewhere—did you mean it?"

He had inhaled. He'd looked away. There had been a long moment where she'd scarcely been able to breathe. His knuckles had turned almost pale, clenching so hard. Very quietly, he'd spoken. "Yes."

One word, and it had ended everything. All her lies. All her wishes. All her dreams.

Crash had been the lie she told herself.

Who does it hurt?

Her. It hurt her. It had stabbed her so deeply she thought she might weep blood.

"Don't wait two months." She had shut her eyes. "Go to France."

"But—"

"There are telegrams," she had told him. "If I have need of you, I will let you know. Go to France. We shouldn't see each other any longer. Now get out."

He had left the room. She'd dressed, her hands shaking, and let herself out.

Part of her had hoped that something would come of that single time together. She'd woken at night, her fingers probing her stomach, not sure if she feared a pregnancy or wanted one. If she'd been with child, she would have been forced to speak with him again, forced to lie herself back into love. But that wish, too, hadn't come true.

She hadn't seen him for months.

He had come back, wild as ever, smiling, with that damned velocipede and his damned plan. He hadn't been hurt at all. But every time she saw him, she still bled.

He was right. His words had only been harsh and painful because they'd been true. She was, as these things were reckoned, a complete waste of a woman. No money. No family. Nothing to give to a marriage but a beauty that would fade in a matter of years.

Crash reminded her of the truth. Of course it hurt to look at him.

And what had she done to deserve his cutting words? She'd forgiven him.

For taking wagers.

For that.

You forgive me for being a bastard, I suppose.

She stopped, coming back to herself from her reverie. She was in the shop where she worked. The day was winding down, slowly, surely. She had only a handful of flowers left, sitting forlornly in empty buckets.

You know I do, she had told him.

You surely forgive me for having the stones to believe I'm worth something.

Yes, she hadn't delivered her sentiments properly. Who could choose the perfect words at a time like that? But Crash was invulnerable. She'd heard him laugh at constables when they'd shoved him against a wall.

He was arrogant, full of himself, confident, audacious…

And she could see him as he had been yesterday glaring at her.

I am good at going fast, he had said. *So good that sometimes all everyone sees is a blur.*

He was right. She *had* known that. She'd known beneath that brash exterior that he was kind. Devoted to his aunt. Boastful, yes, and ambitious, but he'd caught her up in his ambitions, making her feel she could do anything.

Yes, she'd heard him laugh off far worse insults. He'd always laughed the hardest at the cruelest ones. His laughter, like his wickedness, was a persona he put on. He never let anyone know how he really felt.

Anyone, that was, except her.

All this time, she'd felt her own hurt. It had been so all-encompassing that she hadn't heard his.

She had forgiven him for existing, and when he'd complained, she told him he couldn't be hurt by it. How must that have felt? To have had Daisy shrug off his pain as inconsequential simply because he was good at hiding it?

All she'd seen was the blur of speed. The illusion of him that he cast. She'd thought that his laughter made him invulnerable. She hadn't seen him, not really, not even in the moments when he'd stood still for her.

Daisy exhaled and felt the world around her coming into sharp relief. For the first time since Crash had walked away from her, she understood why.

Chapter 6

Crash stood at the narrow window of his aunt's flat. Aunt Ree was bundled up in her seat, her feet warmed by bricks, her eyes narrowed on the street in front of them.

"Did that man just hug a goat?"

Crash found the person she was speaking about, a tall, thin man. "Ah, that's George Mirring. And no, I suspect it wasn't a hug, knowing his habits. It was likely more of a glancing embrace. He tends to be private with his affections."

"Hmm." Her eyes narrowed. "You're making this up."

He didn't let so much as a smile touch his lips. "That goat saved his life once."

She turned to look at him. "Did it?" Her words conveyed the utmost disbelief.

"Here's a little known fact. Goats are excellent watch-creatures. Better even than dogs."

"Crash," Ree said with a shake of her head, "are you capable of speaking without making up a story?"

"I wasn't!" Crash smiled at her. "This is the truth. Mirring got the goat because its nan rejected it. Everyone had given up on getting it to eat, and he raised it from a bottle and a rag. After that, the goat followed him around everywhere. They were nearly inseparable. One day, a man tried to cosh him over the head. The goat grabbed hold of his would-be assailant's coat and held him back."

"And did you see this?"

"No," Crash admitted, "and the goat ate the coat, so there isn't any evidence. But—"

A knock sounded on her door, and they both turned to look in its direction.

"You have a visitor," Crash said slowly.

"How exciting." A glimmer of a smile showed on Ree's face. "Maybe it will be a goat. My very own personal watch-goat. Since they are so very much in vogue these days."

Crash went to the door and opened it. There on the other side stood Daisy.

She looked weary. She looked beautiful. Her eyes were wide, her hair slipping out from under her bonnet. She must have been awake since the early hours of the morning.

She looked up as the door opened, and when she saw it was him, she gave him her shop girl smile—the one that occupied her lips, but not her heart, the one that was all faked politeness. It was the smile she'd give a man who was dallying in her shop at the end of the day.

It was an act. She'd always fooled him with the way she looked: so carefree, with that smile that said she was up to mischief. He'd let that lead him astray. He'd let himself make no such mistakes any longer.

"Ah." He met her eyes. "How appropriate. We were just speaking of goats."

He really shouldn't goad Daisy. He knew he oughtn't. He knew it was unkind, unfair—every *un* he should avoid. But he'd waited and waited for her. He'd expected that telegram in France every day for months.

I'm sorry. I need you. I love you.

He'd come back to discover that in his absence, she'd found another sweetheart.

So yes, he was annoyed with Daisy Whitlaw. Annoyed, frustrated, and…

Her chin squared. There was no mischief dancing in her eyes now. Just a fierce determination. She cradled a brown paper package in her two hands.

"Here," she said. "I hope you'll excuse my calling on you without a prior appointment, but Mr. Lotting said that you were here with your aunt. This is for her."

His eyebrows rose.

She pushed the package into his hands. "You were right," she said simply. "I feel terrible. I was angry about everything you said to me. I never thought through what I said to you. I…" She paused, then the false smile fell from her face. Her tone lowered. "I told you that I would forgive you for who you were, for what you did. That was unfair. It wasn't even true. I *didn't* forgive you. I was still sniping at you about those other things, even last week, which I oughtn't have done if I had actually forgiven you." She frowned and looked down. "I thought nothing could hurt you. I didn't realize that I could."

Crash could not have been more stunned.

Her cheeks were pink with emotion; she wouldn't meet his eyes. "I think I am discovering that I'm something of a horrid person who lies to herself. You were right about that, too."

"Daisy."

"No, don't stop me. I can't stop, or I'll fall." Her words came out in a rapid stream. "I lie to myself. I lie to myself all the time. I would apologize, but I don't know how to stop. Women like me don't get wishes granted. Instead we just keep making them and making them and making them, and what else am I to do…" She trailed off. "So." She shook her head. "In any event, there. I'm sorry."

His fingers closed around the package as she unceremoniously dumped it in his hand.

"Good-bye." She turned to go.

He reached out and took hold of her elbow. "Wait. Daisy. That's all. Really?"

"Really." Her cheeks turned an even brighter red. "Now, if you'll excuse me, I'm going to go…" She pointed out the door.

"You're going to go where?" He felt somewhat stupid.

"Out there," she said. "Just because you were right doesn't mean I want to spend time with you. I may be a waste, but I'm *my* waste, thank you. Good-bye." She said that last in a tone that brooked no denial. "I'll see you for our appointment tomorrow, still, because I haven't stopped lying to myself. I can't appear to give up on anything."

He let go of her, and she turned and marched down the stairs.

He stared after her, his mind whirling. Of all the things he'd ever expected to happen, having Daisy apologize to him…

"What on earth was *that?*" Ree asked behind him.

Crash sighed and let the door close. "That was…a woman."

"A woman." His aunt said the words with care. "And does this woman have a *name?*"

"Daisy," he muttered. "Daisy Whitlaw."

"Ah. *That* woman. The one you said I should meet."

"I…possibly, I…." He looked over at his aunt, who was watching him with her head tilted.

"It's like this," he said. "I was smitten with Daisy for a while." He still felt stunned. "She is clever and kind and funny, and she never made me feel that I was beneath her. Not until…" He looked upward. "In any event, I thought we were of like mind. We were taken with each other. Then the inevitable happened, and after that, she found out about some of the things I'd done in the past, and she…"

Ree was watching him with a frown.

"To make a long story short," he said, "we argued. She made it clear what she thought of my past, and I told her she was…" He couldn't say those words. Not to his aunt.

"I heard what she said." Her voice was cold. "You told her she was a waste?"

He'd heard that voice before. Not for years, but that warning tone could still make him shiver. "Aw, Ree. Not like that. It was more in the context of—"

"The context of the *inevitable* happening?" Ree frowned at him. "Do you mean that you had sexual intercourse with her?"

"I…" He frowned. "Yes."

"And she's been brought up to be a good little English girl, hasn't she? Don't lie; I can tell from her accent."

"Yes, but—"

"So that was the context you refer to, then? 'I know I just took your virginity; terribly sorry, but it was a waste of my time.'"

"Oh, for God's sake." He winced. "It wasn't— I didn't— *She* was the one who overreacted in the first place."

"Think of it from her point of view." Ree folded her arms. "She has gentility in her background."

He gave her a curt nod.

"So all her life, everyone has told her the only thing she has of value is her virginity. That she must guard it; that it's the only thing she can sell to safeguard her security. And here you come. You overwhelm her."

"I didn't—"

"Oh, shut up, Crash," his aunt said. "Don't be stupid. Of *course* you overwhelmed her. She told you she loved you, I wager."

He looked down. "Maybe. But I said it back, and—"

"And," his aunt continued inexorably, "you idiot, you removed her of the one thing she'd been told had value, and you went right ahead and made her think everyone else had been right. That without it, she was a waste."

He stared at her, appalled. "It wasn't like that," he said. "It wasn't. There were other things that happened first. I offered to marry her."

"Crash," Ree said, "do shut your mouth and listen. Do you know how *hard* it was to raise you to believe you could be more?"

He stopped.

"Every day," Ree said. "Every moment we had. Your grandmother, your uncle, my friends… Every day we had to sit you down and tell you. 'He doesn't know who you are; he's accusing you of stealing because he can't see you.' Every damned day we had to drum it into you until you believed it."

He put his hands in his pockets.

His aunt wasn't finished. "Do you suppose anyone told her she was worth anything?"

He paused, and for a moment, he didn't know how to answer. "But… She…"

"I'm sure she never had anyone think her a thief just by looking at her," Ree said. "But men have thought her a great many other things. Including a waste."

He had nothing to say to that. His aunt was right.

"So tell me," she said. "Why did you pay attention to Miss Whitlaw in the first place?"

Crash swallowed. "The first time I saw her, she was defending her mother. Her mother has pains." He indicated. "She tries to work, but, well…"

Ree nodded.

"Someone was accosting Daisy. Telling her that if she didn't confront her mother about her malingering, she'd end up walking the streets." He could almost remember that moment. "Daisy threatened to punch him in the kidneys to see if he could work while in pain."

He could still see her, her hands on her hips. *Do you know my mother, or do I? Then stop telling me what she's doing. If you felt pain the way she did, you'd never leave your bed.*

He shrugged and looked over at his aunt. "I…liked that. I wanted it. I wanted someone who was so loyal to me that she'd punch a man. And then I started talking to her, and she was…"

He stopped again.

"She was trying," he said. "So hard, with so little, and I thought, this is someone who can understand what it was like to be me. Finally. To have to try so hard, and to not let anyone know how hard I was trying. And she understood. I thought she did."

"Crash," his aunt said quietly. She didn't offer advice. She didn't tell him he was wrong. She just looked over at him.

For a long moment, neither of them said anything.

He'd been holding on to his anger—righteous anger!—for so long. Daisy had forgiven him his existence, damn it all. She'd been as bad as that lady, telling him he was a sinner because…

No. She hadn't been that bad. He frowned. He had this to complain about. She'd sent him away. She had found someone else.

He had told her she was a waste.

Maybe… Possibly…

Damn it. Under the circumstances, he'd have sent himself away, too.

He exhaled and looked at the package in his hands.

"There," she said. "Now what do you have?"

He didn't know. Slowly, he unwrapped it. Inside was a glass flask labeled *carbolic acid*. An india rubber ball was attached to a tube. He turned the ball and found a little opening.

She had found him a carbolic smoke ball. He had read an advertisement. This was supposed to rid a room of the fumes that caused pneumonia and influenza. He'd looked for one for days.

And Daisy had obtained one for him as an apology.

Oh, God. What was he doing?

Daisy was angry with him. Crash could tell by the way she smiled at him when she saw him the next evening—a cold, glittering smile that came from the quiet reserve of strength she always kept.

She came up to him at the bench near the canal. "I understand how it is supposed to be now." She looked over at his velocipede leaning against a wall. "If you fall," she said, "you get back on and go faster." Her eyes were dark and steady. "You don't think I can do it. Well, if this is my one chance to secure my fate, I should try to go faster."

She'd leave him behind.

"Daisy."

Her eyes cut to him. "I prefer Miss Whitlaw."

"I owe you an apology," he said.

"You owe me at least two." She looked away from him. "Don't worry; that's one debt I don't intend to collect. Now are we going back to the velocipede?"

"No. I wanted to show you something else today." He gestured. "Come. Walk with me. We'll get cold otherwise."

She looked at him a moment, as if considering walking away. Finally, she took a few steps toward him. It was enough. They started down the gravel path, a sedate two feet apart.

"There's a trick my grandmother taught me," Crash said. "She got it from her mother. She told me to imagine I had a bubble around me. When someone said something about me—something harsh and untrue—she told me to push out on my bubble, to shove those words away. Someone said I had shifty eyes and was up to no good? That was *his* thought, not my reality. I had to push it away. I looked like the devil's spawn? That was *their* belief, not my truth. It wasn't inside my bubble, so I could push it all away. Don't let anyone else's rubbish inside your bubble, she would say."

Daisy didn't look at him.

"It was a good trick," Crash said. "And when it became hard to believe that I was good for something, when everyone told me I was destined for the gallows, I just pushed harder. She taught me to let my mistakes just be mistakes. Not an indictment of my character."

"Is that what I need to do?" Daisy asked. "Learn to push those thoughts away?"

"Yes," Crash said. "And…no. Not yet. You see, you got inside my bubble. Back when we were something to each other. You said things, and I reacted the way I always had. I pushed. Hard. I pushed those thoughts away from me the only way I knew how."

She didn't look up at him.

"I sometimes forget how much of me is truly invisible. People have assumed I was wicked since before I could spell my name. They wouldn't hire me on for respectable work, so I decided to use what they thought of me, and make a name for myself as fashionably unrespectable."

Daisy nodded imperceptibly.

"People look at me and think only the devil will care about me. So I laugh off all their insults with my best devil-may-care attitude. I give the impression that nothing can ever hurt me, because that way…" He shrugged. "That way, fewer people try."

She looked up at him. "I didn't understand. I hadn't thought it through. And…" Her eyes glittered just a little. "I think yesterday was the first time I understood that I hurt more than your pride. I *am* sorry."

"So am I." He wanted to take her hand. To tip her chin up. "I was at least as wrong. You didn't have a bubble. You've never had anyone telling you what thoughts you could push away. Yes, you made a mistake. But so did I. All your life, they've been tossing rubbish at you, telling you that you had to believe it. Blaming you for not understanding it was rubbish. That was my mistake. I should have trusted you enough to explain, instead of dumping more garbage on your head."

She bit her lip. "Explain what?"

"You're a woman. Your ambitions are…" He paused, waiting for her to finish his sentence.

Her fingers clamped together and she looked away. "Unwomanly," she said in a quiet, choked voice. "Unattractive. Unappealing."

"There. That's *their* rubbish. Push it away, Daisy. Your ambitions are a fire that will keep anyone worthwhile warm."

"But—"

He held up a finger. "No buts. Push it away. That's theirs. You don't need to keep hold of it anymore, thank you."

She exhaled. "Crash. I don't know."

"They'll hand you a sack of rubbish and then make you apologize for holding putrefying refuse. They act like their rules are holy and moral, but their only rule is that people like me—people like you—must lose."

She looked up at him. "But we *do* lose."

"Not always. Try another one. Tell me what you fear."

"I'm..." She let out a shuddering breath. "I'm only worth anything now because I'm pretty." Her voice shook. "I'm ten years from being too old, too ugly, too *everything*, and if I don't establish myself now, I'll have to leave my mother."

To have a sell-by date, as if she were a notation scrawled on a can of potted meat. To feel that responsibility.

"Push it away. That's false. That's their rubbish. Can you see the truth?"

She didn't say anything, not for a long while. He waited, letting her think.

"In ten years, I'll be just as clever. I'll be me with more experience. Beauty need not matter."

"Almost right. In ten years," Crash said, "you'll still be pretty. Don't let them tell you that youth is a woman's only beauty. That gray hair and wrinkles will rob you of your appeal. It's a load of rubbish. You should meet my aunt. She's beautiful. Push it away, Daisy."

She shut her eyes. "I'm not...worth anything because I'm not a virgin," she said in a low voice.

"Oh, Daisy." That one stung to hear. He did touch her then, setting his hand on her shoulder.

She raised her eyes to his. A sea of hurt reflected in her pupils.

The thing about being raised as he had? He'd thought of what he would do if she were with child. He hadn't given one thought to the fact of her virginity. It was not something his aunts and her friends thought important, except as an afterthought.

"You don't become less for caring. For loving. For existing, for being a person who does all those things."

She looked over at him.

"Push it away," he said. "Push it all away."

"How?" Her hands fluttered once in front of her. "How? How, when everyone says otherwise, do you…" She swallowed.

"Do I what?"

"How do you smile when people say these things to you? How do you laugh and say that you're proud of your background, when…"

Crash looked Daisy in the face. Her chin was tilted down, her eyes turned to the side. "When what?" His voice seemed dangerously low to his ears.

"When you cannot be," she whispered.

Long ago, he'd heard similar words from her as condemnation. He hadn't heard them as a prayer for mercy, nor as a plea for help. But that was what they were.

"I say that I come from a proud line of dock whores and sailors," he said in a low voice, "because I *am* proud."

She swallowed.

"Nobody except my family takes pride in what we are, so we've had to invent it ourselves. I don't know what race I am. I don't know if the question makes any sense. But I know where I come from. My grandmother was born a slave on the island of Tortola. She accompanied the trader who held her on his voyages as…never mind. One day, a mile from the shore of England, she jumped overboard."

"Why?"

He managed a short, frowning glance. "Because slavery was not recognized in England," he said shortly. "She couldn't swim. She made it to shore anyway. At the time, she was pregnant with my aunt."

Daisy looked up at him.

"When people hear 'dock whore,' they imagine some poor specimen of a woman who wanders up and down the wharf, thinking of nothing but her next john. My grandmother took in laundry. She sewed. She did all these things for sailors, and one of them fell in love with her. How could he not?" He smiled. "The only people who called her a whore were ladies who had no other words for a poor woman with a prior bastard child. My grandfather was an Indian lascar who had been abandoned in London by a shipping company because he had injured his knee. No clergy would solemnify their marriage. It didn't lessen the affection in it. The gentry saw her as nothing but a prostitute. But those of us who knew her? She was an extraordinary woman. I was ten when she died, and the crowd at her funeral wouldn't fit in the tavern."

Daisy let out a long breath.

"My mother, they told me, was sweet. She worked for a seamstress and lived with my grandmother. And yes, I suppose she was a whore, too, in the sense that she took coin in exchange for intercourse from more than one man. But nothing is simple. The life of a sailor is hard. They see no women for months on end; they're expected to be tough as nails all the time. My mother was the shoulder they cried on, the woman they imagined during the worst storms. She was the one who held them and reminded them that they were human, that they mattered. Men would give her everything they had—not to purchase her favors, but because she *was* everything they had. She died when I was two. I have no memory of her, but I remember men coming to our flat for years after, asking after her. I remember them weeping inconsolably when they were told she had passed away." Crash shrugged. "More than one of those men claimed to be my father. He was probably from China, but there was a man from Portugal, and a French fellow… Well, never mind. Three men claimed they were my father, and every time they docked, they'd come see me. They brought me toys and books. They'd leave their earnings with my aunt for my care. They taught me to cheat at cards. They all knew about each other, but they didn't care."

She was watching him with wide eyes. Listening.

"So there you have it, Daisy," he said. "My grandmother was a woman so strong of will that she threw herself over the side of a ship, not knowing how to swim, because she would be free. My mother was a woman so loved that she gave me three fathers after her death, not just one. And my aunt was the one who told me about them—story after story when they had passed away. Every time someone told me to keep my head down or slapped me for thinking myself above my station, my aunt was there. Holding me. Whispering to me that they were wrong, that the blood in my veins was every bit as red as theirs. That I was worth something. Anything."

Daisy looked down.

"I am descended," Crash said, "from a line of dock whores and sailors. Men and women who were told they were nothing. They refused to accept the label. Yes, Daisy, I'm proud."

She exhaled.

"I should never have called you a waste."

Daisy was still considering her feet. "Now what?" she said. Her eyes drifted to the dingy water of the canal. Her question encompassed not just the next hour, but…more. "Now do I get on the velocipede and ride fast?"

"Now," he said, "now you give the speech you intend to deliver at the final competition in a few days. This time, you don't waver. You don't stop. You don't apologize. You believe that you're right, that you can win, that you *deserve it*. And you don't let up."

Chapter 7

It should not have been so exhausting to deliver a speech Daisy had already memorized to an audience of one. But with Crash listening, Daisy heard her words with a new ear.

Everything she said came out sounding stilted and wrong. She could hardly make it through a sentence without an interruption.

"Even though women—"

"You're apologizing," Crash told her. "Stop apologizing for having a store for women."

She swallowed. "Because women are the main clientele, I expect loyalty, word-of-mouth sales, and…" She trailed off. "And a savvy eye for bargains?"

"Reasonable," Crash said, "but why are you asking me a question?"

Her hands curled into fists. Two sentences later…

"Although the main clientele will be—"

"Although?" Crash folded his arms and raised a disapproving eyebrow. "Don't apologize. Start over."

By the time she'd run through it all once, she wanted to scream.

"Good," he said. "Now do it again, this time without prompting."

At the end of the second time through, she wanted to pull out her hair.

"Excellent," Crash said. "Now do it, imagining that you're on a velocipede. All arrogance; no hesitation. Start."

By the fifth time around, she wanted to pull *his* hair out. Even Crash had begun to look weary. His eyelids drooped a little.

She looked at the flickering street lamps. "I must be going," she said. "You've done enough. You must be exhausted."

He gave her a tired smile. "Don't worry about me. I'm game for another five rounds. Never let anyone say I'm anything other than indefatigable."

"But I have to go now."

"Tomorrow, then." He frowned. "No. Tomorrow I've appointments to see more space for my velocipede shop. Friday, although that's cutting it rather close."

"Friday. And now, my mother will be wondering where I am. Good heavens. You must really want to win those wagers."

He frowned at her and looked away. Then he gave his head a tired shake. "I didn't take wagers, Daisy."

Her mind went blank. Of course he had taken wagers on the competition. His entire point in assisting her was to make a little money. He had to… She couldn't… Feelings swarmed her, assailing her from all sides.

"You said." The words came out all choked up. "You *said*, you told me, that people placed bets on the competition."

"Technically," he said, looking upward, "I merely *implied* they had done so and let you come to a false conclusion."

A hard lump formed in her throat.

"But we've never much been technical, have we, Daisy?" He gave her a weary half-smile. "Yes, if you want to put it that way. I lied to you. Of course I didn't make wagers. It would be wrong for me to take bets as if I were an independent observer and then try to influence the outcome. You should know that."

She couldn't help herself. She was exhausted, emotionally drained, and... She began to laugh. "Most people would say that it was wrong to make bets where a woman was involved. That's your reason why you didn't? You have the strangest version of morality I have ever heard."

He looked honestly confused. "Is it supposed to be a *compliment* for me to say that I'd not risk my money on you? I didn't wager because... Oh, for God's sake, I'm not going to explain it now. I just didn't." He shook his head. "English morality is utterly ridiculous. It doesn't make a lick of logical sense."

Talking to Crash about morality was like talking to a wall. You could never talk the wall down, and no matter how you bounced things off it, it always stayed right where it was. Immovable. Unchanged. After an hour of shouting, one was left with the distinct impression that the wall was probably in the right place to begin with. Crash made the rest of the world seem utterly mad in comparison.

Maybe it was.

They stood in silence, Daisy not wanting to speak. She had too many questions. *Why didn't you take the bets? If it wasn't the wager, why did you intervene? Why are you here?* It was the last question she most wanted answered, and he wasn't talking.

"Why?" She made sure her voice didn't shake. "Why did you..."

"Why did I lie to you?" He shrugged. "Well, that's easy. I was fairly certain that if I told you the truth, you wouldn't want my help."

"Crash." She tried to imbue the single syllable of his name with the deepest reprimand.

"Daisy." He didn't mirror her tone. He said her name quietly. Once before, he had used to say her name like that. Like her name was a precious thing, an important thing. Like those two syllables were an honor on his lips.

She couldn't look at him. "If you knew I didn't want your help, you should have…"

"What," he said, "done nothing? I suppose I should have let it go. But I am notoriously terrible at letting things go."

She understood precisely what he was telling her. She'd walked away from him, and nobody had ever done that. He wanted her the way she'd once been—silly, unwise, willing to throw over all good sense when he tossed a smile in her direction. And she, fool that she was, could feel herself falling back into her old ridiculous yearning.

This is not going to happen. This was the moment when she should bar her shutters and wait out the storm.

She was tired.

"It was simple," he said. "If you want to know why I did it, it's because of your sweetheart."

This brought her up short. She turned to him, frowning. "My *sweetheart?*"

"Yes, your sweetheart." He looked in her eyes. "I wanted to… Well, that is…" He frowned. "Maybe I wanted you to miss me a little. I used to imagine him forgiving you for who you are. It made me angry. I wanted you to know you were wrong. That neither you nor I needed forgiveness."

She felt her throat close.

"What are you talking about?" she finally managed to say.

He frowned at her. "You must be exhausted." He sounded patient. "We're talking about your fiancé, Daisy. The man you're supposed to marry? How hard is it to understand that I want you to be happy? That I think he should care about you?"

She felt utterly stricken. She had no fiancé, and the one she would eventually try to acquire would, by necessity, not know her at all.

What came out of her mouth was this: "Crash. You *idiot.*"

"What?"

She took a step toward him.

"You colossal, stupid, ridiculous—" She'd run out of adjectives, but she still had nothing to say to him. "Don't pretend to be a fool. You know."

"What do I know?"

She snapped off the next words. "You *know* I made him up. There is no sweetheart. There is nobody waiting for me. There isn't anyone who cares what I do aside from my mother."

He stared at her in such dazed incomprehension that she wanted to slap him.

"You knew it," she told him. "I told you, and you looked at me just like that, and you said, 'Of *course* I believe you.'"

"Of course I said I believed you," he said stupidly. "Because *of course* I believed you. Why wouldn't you have a sweetheart? Why wouldn't some officer out there—" He jerked his thumb in the vague direction of what might have been Portsmouth "—dream of you every night, and want you to be his? It sounded perfectly reasonable to me."

"Look at me." She gestured. "Oh my God, Crash, *look* at me."

"I am." He frowned at her. "I have. And I know you hate to admit it, but we've known each other quite a while. I know you extremely well. You're lovely. You're loyal. You're funny, and you always put the best face on anything bad that comes your way. Who wouldn't want you?"

"You must think I'm the most gullible woman on the planet."

"Wait one moment," he said. "Are you honestly telling me you *don't* have a sweetheart?"

It took her a moment to realize that he was serious. That all this time, he'd thought... He had actually thought...

He was frowning now. "I returned. I sought you out. You thought you had to *lie* to me about having a sweetheart to keep me away? Did you not think I would listen to you? Did you not trust me? Were you afraid of me?"

"Always," Daisy said. "Every day. Every time I saw you."

He looked surprised. "Daisy, I was an ass. But I would never force myself on you. If I have somehow allowed you to believe otherwise—"

She couldn't listen to him any longer. "I was afraid," she said, "that I would do this." She stepped close, wrapped her hands in his coat lapels, and drew herself up.

One instant, when she felt his shocked breath against her lips. One crazed instant, where she wondered what she was doing—and why—and then she imagined herself on a velocipede, heading pell-mell down the street at top speed.

So she kissed him. She didn't hold back. All the months of hurt, of pain, of loneliness poured out in her kiss. In the feel of his chest against the palms of her hand, his body, radiating warmth against her.

His arms wrapped around her, holding her close. His mouth opened to hers.

God, she'd missed kissing him. Missed the taste of him, that mix of coal-smoke and spice. The all-encompassing feel of his hand on her spine, drawing her in.

She'd missed the brush of his lips, the way he drew her bottom lip in his mouth and bit it, lightly, before he descended on her again. She'd missed feeling beautiful and strong and desired.

She'd missed feeling his heart beat faster, knowing that *she* was affecting him. She'd missed him, and they'd hurt each other so much, and maybe…

She pulled away. He was looking down at her, his eyes dark with desire. Their kiss had turned into a question, the question she hadn't answered yet for herself. Letting this moment linger on would make her response irrevocable. She was tired and upset and…

And she needed time, time to think it all through.

"My mother is waiting," she said.

"I know."

"I'm sorry—" She bit off that apology. "No, never mind. I'm clearly in need of more practice on that front. Let me start again: I refuse to apologize for kissing you."

The corner of one lip tilted up. "Nicely done, Daisy."

"Good day, sir." She stepped out of the circle of his arms.

"Friday, then?" he called after her. "After you finish at the shop? You need to practice more, and…"

He paused. How was it that she could *hear* him smirking in silence?

"And you should spend more time not apologizing to me, I think."

Daisy let out a long breath. "Crash, you're terrible."

"No, I'm not," he said, sounding amused. "I'm brilliant at everything. And if you would like to not apologize to me in that particular manner once again, I'll be happy to accommodate you."

She tossed her head. "Go smoke your head. I believe you have the medical apparatus for that now."

His laugh chased her down the street—warm, inviting, and not the least bit apologetic.

Them sun had set by the time Daisy arrived home. Her skin was numb from the cold; she rubbed her hands together in the dark hall before her door, peeling her gloves away, stamping her feet until the feeling returned.

Her lips still tingled. And her heart…

Just as well her mother wasn't home; her face would give away all her secrets. She opened the door into darkness and reached for the matches.

"Daisy." Her name came from the bed.

"Oh, Mama." Daisy let the wooden match fall back into its box. "I didn't know you were home."

"Just getting a little rest." Her mother started to sit up.

Daisy rushed over. "There's no need to stir on my account. I'll manage supper for you tonight."

"You do too much for me."

Daisy didn't answer as she sliced and buttered bread.

Deep down, sometimes she agreed. She had told herself she was a good daughter. But as she set the teakettle on the hob, she wasn't sure anymore.

The future was coming. She ought to have felt a pit of dread in her stomach at that. Maybe, tonight, she was too weary to worry.

Or maybe she was thinking of Crash.

How can you be proud? she had asked Crash. And he'd answered. Oh, how he'd answered.

She'd never asked that question of herself.

How can I be proud?

"You taught me to read when I was five," Daisy said slowly.

Her mother frowned at her in the gloom. Daisy walked over to the bed and sat down. "You taught me how to jab a man who brushed up against me on the omnibus with a hat pin when nobody was looking." Her voice was shaking. "You drilled me in proper speech because you told me I'd have better prospects if I could sound genteel. You make dinner and handle laundry and do more than your fair share of lacework."

"Daisy. What are you saying?"

Daisy took her mother's hand. "You taught me to never stop. To always try one last thing. To keep hoping through the bleakest of times."

Daisy had not let herself truly want to win the competition, not until this moment. Or maybe it was that deep down, she had always wanted to win. She'd wanted it so much, with every aching fiber of her being, that she hadn't let herself know the ferocity of her desire. She had told herself she couldn't do it instead to cushion her heart from the blow.

Now she thought about what her emporium would mean. If she succeeded, she'd have not just financial security and a lasting position. It would be a place where her mother might help, as much as she could, with no employer to scold her when her rheumatism took a turn for the worst. She could have a chair in front of the fire on bad days, and Daisy could work and still see to her needs.

Daisy had not let herself feel her desire until this moment. Now, she wanted. She wanted the shop in her imagination fiercely.

"Daisy," her mother said. "What are you saying?"

Daisy's voice trembled. "Papa gave up when he lost the store all those years ago. You? You never did. You are the reason I am here. Alive. Well. Taking care of you."

Her mother said nothing.

"And so nothing more of the future," Daisy said. "If you please. *Whether* I marry, I promise you, Mama, you will always have a place with me. No matter how hard I must try. No matter how many times I have to stretch for plans outside my grasp. No matter how many times I am told no. I am proud of you. I'm proud of who you made of me. And I'm not going to stop being proud, no matter what the future brings."

"Daisy." Her mother took her hand.

Daisy couldn't win the competition. She had told herself that for so long that she had made herself believe it. But Crash had been right. The grocer's certainty that she would fail? That was his rubbish. The reason she kept reaching was because she could not stop dreaming.

She wouldn't.

"Daisy." Her mother's voice was small. "I'm proud of you, too."

Daisy's chin went up. "Good. Then watch what I can do."

Chapter 8

Daisy was counting out the final coins in the till two days later, going through her speech for the competition on the morrow, grimly preparing herself to do her very best. The door opened. A gust of cool wind swept in, and she looked up.

The momentary annoyance at a customer arriving right at closing was swept away when she saw who it was.

"Crash." She tried not to smile. "I didn't expect you to meet me here."

"No?" He slid his gloves off and sauntered toward her. And oh, did he saunter. Nobody could saunter like Crash, with those languid steps, that slight roll to his hips. She hadn't known what a saunter truly was until she'd met him.

The fact that it left her staring inadvertently at his crotch…

She swallowed and dragged her gaze to his face.

He came up to her, so close that he could reach out and touch her. And he did. He set his hand atop hers where it rested on the till. A little thrill ran through her.

"You need to practice your speech again," he said in a matter-of-fact tone.

A strangled noise escaped her.

"Yes," he said in a low, warm voice. "You do. I know you're exhausted and I know that two days ago, I tried my damned best to rattle you. Now you need to do it one more time—once when I *don't* try to rattle you. You need to do it perfectly once, so you know how that feels."

"Crash." She should say no. Spending time with him was dangerous; it always had been. "It's so cold today. The thought of trying to be perfect while my hands freeze next to the canal…"

Speaking of hands. His hand twitched atop hers. "Luckily," he said in a low voice, "I have a perfectly warm set of rooms. With tea. And I can obtain pastries."

"I will not be won over by baked goods." Daisy folded her arms.

"Yes, but what about pastries *and* tea?" He waggled an eyebrow at her.

"No self-respecting woman would…" She paused and listened to her own words. Come to think of it, why wouldn't a self-respecting woman go into a room with a man she wanted to be alone with? Especially with pastries. She was tired; she couldn't think straight. And she was always ravenous after work.

It didn't sound like a terrible idea.

He waited, watching her.

"You know," she said severely, "this whole questioning of societal mores thing… It's entirely self-serving on your part, I've just realized."

"Come to my side," he murmured. "We have baked goods and tea."

"That's a terrible argument. The side of proper English morality also has pastries and tea. They practically invented it."

"They stole the tea, and they certainly never baked the biscuits. In addition, I know fifteen ways to give a woman an orgasm."

Daisy choked.

"Which is rather antithetical to their position. So which do you prefer, Daisy. Pastries and tea? Or pastries, tea, and, orgasms?"

"I'll have tea," Daisy said, "and…a baked good or two." She felt her cheeks burn. "But if we are going to be precise about the matter, your presence is not necessary for me to have any of those things. I can manage all three on my own."

His eyes met hers and he let out a long breath. "Bravo, Daisy." He pulled his hand away. "Now there's an image. Damn."

She locked the shop and gathered the final remnants of flower stems. "I have to take out the rubbish."

He slid ahead of her and picked up the basket. "Toss it out, then."

She gave him a look. Oh, she tried to make it a warning, repressive look, but her smile got in the way. "Don't think I'll be won over so easily. I value myself more than a biscuit or two."

"What do you want, then?"

"What do you think?" Daisy shrugged. "To get on your velocipede, and to aim straight for the walls. As fast as I can go." She took the rubbish bin from him. "You can sit in one place and listen to my speech."

They stopped at the bakery. Crash chose little twists of puff pastry laced with cinnamon; Daisy asked for currant scones. They went back to his rooms in good cheer. She smiled at him the whole way.

This is what it would be like, his mind whispered. *This is what it would be like if we were together. If…*

No. When.

Daisy gave her speech. He didn't interrupt. He wished her all the best in the world, pouring every ounce of good will into his smile.

"You're brilliant," Crash said when she finished.

"No," Daisy started to say. Then she paused. Crash could see her inhale. She tilted her head. Then she gave him a glowing smile. "I *was* brilliant, wasn't I? At first, I thought I couldn't be any good in comparison. Now, I think I'm excellent. What are you doing to me?"

"Nothing. You're amazing on your own, you know. You've always known, deep down, that you deserved more. Now you want others to believe they deserve it, too. That's what you're really selling in your emporium."

There was something about having her stand above him as he sat in his chair. His head tilted back and his body came alive. Stirring. Wanting.

She looked at him for a moment, then gave a slow nod. "That *is* what I'm selling."

"And I," Crash continued, "for one, bow to your genius."

One of her eyebrows rose in a perfect arch. She took a step toward him. "Do you, now?"

"I positively genuflect to it. In fact, I—"

Daisy held up a hand. "All talk. I've had tea and scones. You didn't promise me adulation, Crash. You promised…"

She trailed off, and Crash found himself holding his breath, waiting for her to say the word.

"You promised…"

"I promised you an orgasm? Oh, no." He sat back in his chair and folded his arms. "You declined. I recall you promising to see to your own."

Her eyes narrowed. "Are you asking me to leave?"

He paused. He considered. Then he crooked a finger at her. "On second thought… Come here."

She took a step toward him, then another, until she stood next to his chair. He sat watching her. Wondering what she would do. Hoping…

She didn't reach out. She didn't lay a hand against his cheek. She looked at him with solemn blue eyes. He wondered, then, if she was remembering what had happened the last time they'd been in this situation—alone together, their bodies humming, reason taking its leave.

There had been nothing quite so vulnerable as that moment after they'd had each other, when passion was sated, when the future had opened up before them as a vast unknown. They'd wounded each other deeply then.

"Not again," he said slowly.

She looked at him.

"I promise," he said. "Not again. No matter what happens. I will never again lash out at you in anger. I will never tell you the words that other people would say. I will never say you're less because I've been hurt. I promise."

"I promise," she said. "I will never again see you with anyone else's eyes. Just mine."

Their eyes met. Those promise settled on him like a comforting weight. They felt like a velvet cloak in the middle of a winter night, shielding him from winds and cold.

"I'm sorry," he said, "that I hurt you. So much that you shoved me away."

She reached out and took his hands. "Make it better, then."

He wasn't sure if he pulled her onto his lap or if she came to settle there on her own. This time, when he kissed her, he kissed her for all his hopes, all his wishes. For the future he'd built. For the things he wanted for him. For *them*.

His hand slid up her spine. Gently.

She moved to straddle him, her thighs settling against his hips. Even through layers of petticoat and skirt and trousers, he could feel her body press against him. Against his cock, which slowly came to life.

They'd done this before, kissing, touching, exploring until they were both afire. This time, though, it felt… fragile, like a plant thought dead, poking new leaves through the soil after a freezing winter. Fragile and yet strangely robust, as if the roots had grown deep during their dormancy.

He kissed her gently, nurturing every unfurling leaf.

The gasp she made as he kissed her. The lift of her head as he pressed his lips to her neck, turning her face up like a flower to the sun. The parting of her lips as his hand found her nipple.

"There you are, Daisy," he whispered. "There you are."

Her hands slid down his ribs. "Here you are." Their lips met once more.

"Here." His hands slid up her skirt, skimming the soft flesh of her knees, her thighs. "Let me help."

She was wet; when he slid his thumb between her folds, her breath caught momentarily. That little catch nearly broke him. He kissed the side of her neck, wanting more. She tilted her head back.

"There?" he asked.

"Yes." The word came out in a hush. "There."

"Wait."

"Wait? I can't—"

He bodily picked her up, holding her close. "If I set you on the bed, I can use both hands instead of just the one."

She nodded, and he brought her there. He could smell her desire, the wet, intoxicating musk of arousal. He set her down, lay beside her, and kissed her again. A kiss on the lips; a brush of his hand back between her legs. She opened for him, mouth and body alike. Her hips moved against his touch.

"This is why I need my other hand." He unlaced her bodice, freeing her breasts.

She froze when his lips found her nipple, but then exhaled and moved against him. They found a rhythm like that, her beside him, his hand between her legs.

Her breath grew faster, then faster still. Then she let out a little choking noise.

God, he'd missed her. Her fingers clamped on his arms; her passage clasped his fingers, and her hips moved in time with him. She came apart in his arms.

He wanted more. All of her. That dazed look in her eyes, that soft, sweet smile that she gave him. He wanted to do it all over, to go back to the last time he had this, to do it right this time.

Her skin was warm; her mouth was soft and inviting when she kissed him.

More. His body was hard and all too ready. *Don't think. Act.*

"Daisy." His voice was low. "Darling. We have to talk of what comes next."

"No." She smiled up at him. "We don't."

"We haven't decided anything. We should—"

She reached up and pulled him to her, and all his *shoulds* went up in smoke. There was nothing but Daisy, her hands pulling the tails of his shirt from his trousers. Her fingers ran up his chest, and it became imperative that he disrobe. That they touch each other. That the next kiss, when he took it, be skin to skin with nothing between them.

He shed his clothing and slid back against her. He could feel the curve of her hips against him, the nubs of her nipples against his chest. His cock nestled against her, hard and wanting, and he could not help that tiny thrust of his hips. God, he needed to think.

He pulled away six inches.

"Crash." Her hair was spilled on the sheets; her eyes were wide and inviting.

"Daisy, dearest."

He'd been here before, with her. Wanting her so badly. *Needing* her.

Now he wanted to redo it. To take that hurt he'd given her last time and turn it to pleasure. Nothing but pleasure for her from here on out.

Even now, even with his blood insistently thrumming in his veins, with his desire riding high, he wanted to cuddle her close, to build a fortress with his body to keep the world from getting at her.

He couldn't shield her from everything. He hadn't even been able to shield her from herself.

She smiled and curled her finger at him, beckoning him closer.

And in that moment, he was helpless. He leaned his head down to her. "Daisy. We shouldn't."

She laughed. "Who are you," she said, "and what have you done with my Crash? You sound like someone who cares about such things as propriety and manners. We should, and you know it."

They should.

He knew it.

He kissed her again, longer this time, lingering. He let his hands slide down the sides of her body, let his knees nudge hers further apart. Her breath scattered.

He slid inside her.

"Oh, God." The words fell from her lips.

"Sweetheart."

She surrounded him, all warmth and tight surrender. He took her, slow sweet inch by slow sweet inch, waiting for her breath to loosen before he went further. She opened to him slowly. Perfectly.

Until they were together, until he was buried deep inside her, her legs wrapping around his hips. Until she smiled up at him, and he wanted this, nothing but this, forever, and he drove into her, gently at first, then harder still. Until the world began to break apart. He held that line, waiting, bringing her with him, until they both dissolved in pleasure.

He held her afterward. He didn't ever want to let go. He felt soft and vulnerable and almost afraid of what might come next.

But they had to disengage. They had to lie next to one another.

They had to look in each other's eyes. He had to stroke her cheek and say the words that he most feared. "Daisy, darling. We have to talk of the future."

She exhaled, leaning her forehead against his. "The final round of the competition is tomorrow. I don't know how to think beyond it."

And yet beyond it was where they had to go.

The truth, sometimes, was a weapon. He didn't want to wound her, but...

He exhaled. "We both know you should win. We know it."

But. That last word went unspoken.

She looked him in the eyes. "We both know I won't."

He shut his eyes.

"I'm not stupid," Daisy said. "Just ambitious."

"If we'd found ourselves here together, earlier," Crash said, "things might be different. I'd saved money, you know. But I've already committed what funds I have to a first order of velocipedes. They'll arrive in two months, and what I have left needs to be spent a lease. If I had known then, I might have made different choices. But if tomorrow goes as…"

He couldn't make himself say it.

Daisy sat up. "You were right," she said. "You were entirely right when you told me I lied to myself."

"No, Daisy…"

She didn't look at him. "I've spent all these years telling myself I won't get my wishes. My little game with Judith saved me from disappointment. It let me label my every wish as foolish and insubstantial. Impossible. A game. A dream of things that would never come to pass. I believed I would never get anything I wanted."

"That won't happen. I won't let it happen."

She folded her arms around her legs.

"No. *I* won't let it happen. This wish, Crash?" Her voice shook. "This one? This wish for Daisy's Emporium? I tried not to let it sink its hooks into me. I tried not to want it too hard. But it's too late. I want it. I want it so much I can taste it."

He slid toward her, putting his arm around her.

"You were telling me that I can believe in you," Daisy said. "That you'd never hurt me. I know you won't. What I don't know is…" Her voice shook. "Is whether I can believe in myself."

"Oh." He hurt, looking at her. "Oh, Daisy."

She gave a little sniff and looked at him. That determined look came into her eye—the one that he'd seen when they'd first met. He'd fallen in love with her then.

"But I will." Her chin squared. "I need to. I need to believe that I can do this. That if I just pedal fast enough, I won't fall. Not this time."

"Daisy."

She set her hand on his shoulder. "I won't come to you feeling myself a failure. I want to prove that I can do this. Ask me what our future holds after I've won my own destiny. Ask me after I've accomplished everything I never believed I could really prove."

He felt a hint of panic. She was walking away. Again. Telling him he wasn't good enough, that he couldn't be enough for her...

"I need to go fast," she said. "I need to pedal with all my might. I cannot go as fast as I need if you are there to hold me up."

"Are you saying that I'll hold you back?"

She looked back at him, not saying a word.

He inhaled, swallowed the indignant response that leapt to his lips. Swallowed the pain. The part of him that wanted to argue, to make her listen, to...

To do what he'd done last time.

He blew out a breath instead. "I think," he said after a moment, "that you also need to know." He swallowed. "Last time we found ourselves here, talking of the future, things went...badly."

Her eyes darted to her hands.

"I think you need to know," he said, "that I won't hurt you again. That this time, I'll listen."

Her eyes widened a moment, and then shut. "Maybe. Maybe that, too."

He slid his arm around her. He didn't want to say the next words. Not with all they could entail. But he had to do it. "I'll never hold you back. Never. Not even if it means letting you go."

He didn't let go, not right away, and she didn't move away. Not for minutes. He did his best to memorize the scent of her, the complex smell of lavender soap and something sweet beneath that. He committed the feel of her skin, smooth and soft, to his store of thoughts. He learned the shape of her in his arms by heart. Just in case.

They sat there, holding one another, until the last bit of sun disappeared from his window, cloaking them in darkness.

"Go, Daisy," he finally said. "Go fast. Don't stop. I'll see you tomorrow after the competition."

Chapter 9

aisy woke on the day of the final presentation in the hours that were too dark to properly be called morning. The world seemed preternaturally still. When she peered through the curtains, the street she looked out on was cloaked in fog.

She could almost pretend the building across the way had vanished. That her entire uncertain future had been swallowed in mist. There was nobody but her, her and her mother. In that moment, winning seemed possible.

Likely, even.

I could win. The thought threaded through her like the bright ribbon she wove through her hair. *I could win.*

This irrational hope did not vanish. Not as the sun crept to the horizon, spilling pink mist down the street. Not as she dressed, doing up her buttons, making sure she looked like a respectable, sober woman who could start a business and succeed.

I could win.

She felt as if she were on a velocipede, the wind whipping around her face as she pedaled with all her might. She felt as if her arms were wings. If she raised them, she might take flight. As long as she went fast enough, she'd never fall.

I could win.

She nurtured her treacherous, dangerous hope as she marched down the streets to the gathering. Those who were headed the same way saw her and whispered behind their hands.

She invented a conversation for them.

Look. That's Miss Daisy Whitlaw. She could win.

When one of them let out a burst of explosive laughter, she smiled and nodded at them. They were laughing because they knew how ridiculous the other men would look when she won.

I can win, she told herself as people filled the square, sitting first on benches, then bunching in groups along the edges. The crowd grew large, then larger still, its noise a hum that tried to slide under her skin.

I can win.

I can win, she repeated as the grocer introduced the contenders. He lingered before introducing her.

"Finally, Mr. Daisy—" He stopped, pausing for the ugly laughter that erupted from the crowd. "Right. It's *Miss* Daisy Whitlaw. Our favorite female."

I can win. She wouldn't let that little witticism destroy her confidence. Not this time. Not again.

I can win, she told herself as the other contenders gave their final speeches. The proposals were much improved over the course of the week, she had to admit. Viable, even. She applauded each one politely. But deep down, she knew the truth.

I can win.

No, more than that.

Mine is better. I should win.

The grocer called her to come to the front, and she squared her jaw.

I will win.

Daisy stood. As she did, the man next to her set his hand on her wrist. Her heart was already pounding; her throat was dry. She looked down at the fingers clawed into her cuff, followed the arm back to the glaring face of Mr. Flisk.

"There are men here with wives and children," he hissed at her. "You're making a spectacle of yourself with your selfishness."

For a second, her throat dried. *Selfishness. Spectacle.*

Then she remembered how to ride a velocipede: look forward and pedal faster. She imagined his words bouncing off a glittering ball that surrounded her. And Daisy pulled her sleeve from his grasp and proceeded to the front.

The crowd seemed a hostile force, more so even than the time before. She looked over the sea of faces. A man in the front sniggered. Behind him, a woman sat with a stony face, her arms crossed in disapproval.

This time, they'd known she was going to be here, and they were prepared. A low murmur of unhappiness rose like a susurrus from the crowd.

It was not all that rose. She saw it coming as if in a dream. A potato flew through the air to splat rottenly on the boards in front of her.

"For shame!" someone called out. "For shame!"

Her stomach gave an involuntary lurch.

But there was nothing to do except go faster. Harder. She inhaled and rolled her shoulders back. Her chin went up an inch. Let them all hate her. She didn't care. Except…

In the first row, a little girl with bright red curls was seated on her father's lap. She was watching the stage, and at the sight of Daisy standing up front, her eyes widened. She tugged her father's sleeve, whispering urgently.

Her father shook his head, but the little girl waved her hands in excitement and gave Daisy a gap-toothed smile.

There, at the very back, Daisy's mother sat, bundled in scarves, smiling as best as she could. Crash stood against one of the back walls, watching her intently.

To the right, in the third row, a young woman gave Daisy a tremulous smile. Two rows down from her sat Mrs. Wilde, wearing a tulip in her buttonhole and leaning forward.

Daisy wasn't entirely alone.

She could win. She *would* win.

She wasn't going to apologize for her existence. She didn't need to be forgiven for her ambition. She wasn't going to pretend she didn't matter to assuage their fears.

Let them throw their rotten produce. Let them tell her she was nothing. Let them call her selfish for wanting the same chance as any man. Daisy didn't care; she was going to win.

She squared her shoulders, reached down, and picked up the potato. It was a slimy, shattered mess.

"Women." She said the word loudly, projecting her words to the entire crowd. She held the potato up. "We all know it's an ugly world out there."

That disapproving murmur faltered just a little bit, and Daisy bulled her way into the temporary silence.

"You have been told all your lives that you are a part of the ugliness," Daisy said. "That your only value is to others. That you must labor on piecework, or bend over a desk copying words, or work a loom in a factory. You've been told your only value is what you make for others. You've been told that you'll lose your beauty and once you do, there's nothing more to you."

"For shame!" someone in the crowd yelled.

Daisy ignored him and went on. "Daisy's Emporium of Handpicked Goods is more than a general store. It's more than a bookseller, or a flower shop, or a tea shop. We'll sell fresh-cut flowers, chosen for their lifespan, so that for a mere halfpenny a week, you'll have something pretty in your life. We will have scarves and gloves that are designed to be splendid as well as serviceable. All these years, you've believed that society has given up on you. And all these years, you've refused to give up on yourself. Daisy's Emporium is for you."

The murmurs had not stopped, but Daisy continued.

"We will have not just goods, but gatherings. For no cost at all, you'll be able to attend a course that will show you how to use a few ribbons to beautify a space, how to make curtains that will make your rooms both warmer and brighter. For those who can't attend, we will sell halfpenny booklets on those same subjects."

Daisy wasn't going to stop now. She was going to win.

"Men." She addressed the crowd. "You are no doubt thinking you have no place at Daisy's Emporium, and I'll grant you the goods I have will be chosen with women in mind. But many of you may wonder about curtains as well, and you'll not be shamed for attending. Daisy's Emporium is for you, too." She took a deep breath. "Now let me lay out the financials of Daisy's Emporium."

"For shame!" someone called again, but repetition had eroded those words of their hurt. This time the call seemed muted.

She went into detail: The cost of goods. The estimates she'd received. The work she would need to do. Where she'd print the booklets. What sort of courses she had planned, and how they'd pay for themselves with sales of tea and goods while still providing additional income for the local women who might teach.

She talked about the number of unmarried women on the parish rolls, and how few of the main businesses on the commercial street were intended to meet their needs.

"I believe," Daisy said in conclusion, "that this is an opportunity to not only establish a business, but to better the surrounding environment. I hope that Daisy's Emporium is chosen for us all."

There was a moment of silence as Daisy gave her final curtsey.

She looked over the crowd—at the little girl in the front, still beaming up at her. At Mrs. Wilde, who gave her a tremulous smile. At the woman in the second row who had stopped frowning and was now looking thoughtfully into the distance.

"Thank you." She turned and swept back to her seat.

"For shame!" someone yelled halfheartedly, but there was a good amount of applause, too. Loud, and more than would come from one or two people being polite.

She'd done well. She knew she had.

Daisy was going to win. She had to believe that to keep the smile on her face. To walk calmly back to her seat with her head held high. She was going to win. Nobody else had gone through parish records to talk about the demand for their business, nobody but her. Nobody else had official estimates from suppliers. Nobody else had a plan anything like hers, and damn it all, if they weren't going to award her the prize, she wanted them to at least be embarrassed by their stupidity.

She sat facing the crowd and smiled. Let them call for her shame; they could call forever. She had no shame in besting everyone else.

She had to stay like that, frozen in place, smiling, for long minutes while the judges conferred. The murmur of the crowd grew to a dull roar as people argued over their favorites.

She'd done well. She *would* smile. She had already won; the only question was whether they would award her the victory or steal it from her hands. She wouldn't let any of them see the slightest crack in her composure.

She sat in place, her hands clenching because her teeth should not.

Finally, the grocer came to the front. "Ladies and gentleman," he said, "after much deliberation, we have reached a near-unanimous decision."

Daisy would not lean forward. She would not scoot to the edge of her seat. She would not hold her breath.

The man turned to gesture at the stage. "Our winner is…"

He let his sentence trail off suggestively, and oh, that was cruel.

Because her imagination slid her name into that gap. *Miss Daisy Whitlaw.* Every fiber of her being yearned to hear that. *Miss Daisy Whitlaw. Say it. Miss Daisy Whitlaw.*

She felt as if she were watching him in a dream. He gestured expansively and spoke. "It's Miss Daisy Whitlaw!"

Her world seemed to fade. It *was* a dream. It had to be. He'd said her name. He had actually said her name.

But it couldn't be a dream. In a dream, his pronouncement would have been met with thunderous applause. Now, the crowd simply murmured in confusion. Someone started clapping madly; Daisy wasn't sure who. But it was just one person.

She didn't care who applauded her or how few. That had been her name. Her name. She'd won. She had really won. It had worked; she had actually won.

Her hopes jumped high, so high. Her heart hammered in her chest.

It wasn't just the money. It wasn't just that she'd won against impossible odds. It was that she'd been brilliant, and they'd been forced to recognize it. She'd fought for her wish, and she had prevailed. The impossible had come to pass.

Daisy felt light-headed. She was not going to faint; she wasn't. She was going to accept the award graciously, sweetly, fairly. She'd make sure they never regretted it.

She started to stand. She'd scarcely stood up from her chair when the grocer let out a loud, wheezing laugh.

"Just a little joke, ladies and gentlemen! I do so love my jokes; I hope you'll forgive me that one. We all know that this esteemed panel could never err in so grotesque a fashion."

Daisy's behind hit her seat. For a moment, she could scarcely breathe. Little spots swam in front of her. The edges of her vision darkened. She swayed in place.

She had to force herself to take one breath, then another. She wasn't going to faint on stage. The cruelty of the man. Raising her hopes up, only to smash them into the ground. Calling her dreams grotesque in front of everyone.

She was not going to cry in front of them all. She *should* have won. She could have won.

She hadn't.

She steeled her chin, planted a smile on her face, and looked ahead. The crowd was a blur.

She scarcely heard the words that followed.

"Mr. A. Flisk," the grocer said, "your plan for a dry-goods store has been selected as the winner of the contest."

Daisy couldn't process the sounds that assailed her. Not the applause, tinged with a derisive note. Not the congratulatory speech the grocer gave, nor the grateful acceptance that Mr. Flisk delivered. She fixed a vacant smile on her face and stared into nothing.

She hadn't won. They hadn't let her.

She waited as hands were shaken, as ribbons were bestowed. She waited until the crowd was dismissed and people began leaving the arena in a great mass.

She didn't want to talk to anyone. Not anyone at all.

She slid behind the stage and slipped through an alley. The street on the other side was bare still; she'd avoided them all. Thank God.

When she was sure nobody could see her, she started running. She didn't stop for a long time.

Chapter 10

Daisy ended up in a park a mile away, her feet hurting, her lungs complaining, and her hands trembling.

She hadn't won.

She'd let herself believe it was possible. She'd put everything she had into the proposal and the presentation. She'd done well—better than anyone else. She knew she had.

She just hadn't done well enough. There could be no *well enough* for the likes of her.

She hadn't won.

She *couldn't* have won. She felt as if she'd lost not only her chance at a future, but at that short-lived confidence Crash had showed her. How could she go to him now? She'd gone as fast as she could and smashed headlong into their laughter and their jokes. She felt splintered into pieces.

She'd been lying to herself. There had never been any way to win. Not ever. She'd been setting herself up for disappointment from the first.

Now that the future she'd let herself desire was torn from her grasp… Now she had to look clearly at what would happen to her.

She could marry. She could likely marry Crash. It was not the drab, suffocating fate she'd once feared. She'd just started hoping for…more.

She looked up. The park was empty, the branches devoid of leaves. The grass underfoot was brown, a hard blanket of ice encrusting the soil. Brick walls, covered with dead ivy, met her gaze. She could feel the future she'd let herself dream of falling from her grasp.

"I might never have any of my dreams. They might all be stolen from me." The sound of her voice rang out in the quiet.

The words were colder than the winter air. She listened to those words. Tasted them, *knew* them, made herself believe them.

When would she learn? She never got her wishes. She'd let herself believe, and she knew how stupid that was. When was she going to learn to stop wishing? How bloody would they have to slap her hands before she finally learned her lesson and gave up?

Her eyes stung, and she looked up at the gray sky. She should just accept what she had. Things were going well with Crash. That was more than she'd hoped even a week ago.

Loving Crash was easy; she'd fallen back into it with an ease that was hardly surprising. She'd scarcely ever stopped.

Loving herself was harder. How long would she have to wait until she stopped yearning for more?

She exhaled into the wind.

How long until she finally gave up? She waited, listening, yearning for the answer. It came on the next breath.

Until she didn't have hands to reach with. Until she lacked a heart to hope with. Until her every wish had been smashed into dust.

She was not made for giving up. Not ever, and especially not *now*.

She had never needed to prove to herself that wishing was futile. When she fell, there was only one thing to do: Get back on and go faster, and faster still.

Daisy inhaled, stilled her hands on her skirts, and started walking.

The chandelier was just as bright, the damask silk paper just as expensive.

But Daisy had changed. She refused to feel out of place in her friend's home, no matter how expensive the furnishings.

"Daisy." Judith came into the room, followed by a maid who did her best not to frown suspiciously at Daisy. Judith, at least, was smiling.

Daisy's heart was pounding, both from the brisk walk and from fear. But she held out her hands to her friend.

"Judith."

Judith took her fingers and grimaced. "You're cold as ice," she said. "What brings you here this fine Saturday evening? If I had known—"

"I know," Daisy interrupted. "You'd have sent the carriage. But I don't need a carriage." She exhaled. "I need…"

Judith motioned for her to sit. "Is everything well? Your mother? Yourself?"

Daisy set the papers she had brought with her on the table. "I entered a…competition. Of a sort. It started a week ago."

Judith looked at her. "You said nothing of this to me."

"I didn't want you to know." Daisy moved the top paper. "If I had, you would have known how much I wanted to win. And if you had known that…"

Daisy held back a moment. If she had told Judith the truth, her friend would have offered to help. Of course she would have. And Daisy would have felt she didn't deserve it.

"You would have known how desperate I felt," Daisy said. "Everything in your life is…" She gestured, an expansive swing of her arm that encompassed the sparkling glass windows, the oil lamps, the crystal chandelier sending gleams of light throughout the room.

Judith frowned. "You felt desperate? And you didn't tell me?"

"I don't want to be the fly in your ointment," Daisy said. "The person you always worry about. You've achieved everything; you shouldn't be bothered with my complaints. I don't want to be the reminder in your life of what you've escaped."

Judith looked at Daisy, her eyebrows drawing down. Slowly, she exhaled. "Daisy."

"I didn't want to leech off you," Daisy said. "I wanted to feel I had something to contribute to our friendship."

"Oh, Daisy. I'm so sorry, so, so sorry. If I've made you feel—"

Daisy shook her head. "I didn't want to burden you with it."

Judith exhaled. Then she motioned Daisy to lean in, and when she did, she whispered. "Daisy. The servants think I'm beneath them."

Daisy looked at her friend. "Your pardon?"

"Everything I do—how I dress, how I eat, how I plan menus—meets with resistance. 'Are you sure, my lady? The dowager wouldn't.' The servants are unfailingly kind and polite, but the reminder that I don't belong is incessant."

Daisy took Judith's hands.

"The servants have been in the family for generations. They mean well. It's getting better, but…" Judith sighed. "Then there are the children. Benedict has gone from telling me he won't go back to school to saying he has no intention of staying in England. Theresa fights with the dowager marchioness *daily*. And we still have no word of Camilla. What is the point of all this when…?" Judith trailed off, then raised her chin. "No, I know what the point is. It will all work itself out. But the transition is…not easy."

"Oh, God." Daisy squeezed her friend's hands. "You never said anything to me. Not one word. Why did you never say anything?"

"How could I complain to you? What was I to say? That I was envious of you? That I wished everything might be simple again?"

They exchanged looks.

"And Christian?" Daisy asked in a low voice.

"As wonderful as ever," Judith said. "He's the only reason I haven't given up and set fire to the building. I thought Theresa would do it; no, it's more likely to be me."

"About that competition," Daisy said. "Fifty pounds was the object; the winner with the best plan for a business was to receive the entire amount. They didn't technically *say* it was for men only."

Judith winced. "Oh dear."

"Precisely," Daisy said. "It turned out about as well as one might imagine. But my plan was sound and…" She slid the papers across the table. "Here. I need a business partner. You provide the capital. I'll provide the labor. We'll split the profits." She glanced at her friend. "I'll ask for forty percent."

"Mmm." Judith picked up the pages and started reading. "Daisy. This will not help my social standing."

"Will it not?" Daisy shrugged. "There's something I've learned in the last few weeks. When you feel yourself on the verge of falling, you need to go faster. To not apologize for who you are, what you have come from. Apologies sound like excuses. You're brilliant, Judith, and kind, and funny, and anyone who does not like you is unworthy of you."

"Easy to say."

"I know." Daisy looked at her friend. "But has giving a damn about them changed how they react to you?"

"No."

"Then why bother giving one?"

Judith frowned. She tilted her head. "Yes," she said thickly. "Yes. And I need a friend. A real friend, a female friend. Christian is wonderful, but I can't go forward without you. Daisy, this is…" She trailed off and waved the papers. "This is brilliant. I love it."

For a moment, Daisy almost contradicted her. Then she remembered what Crash would say about apologizing. She lifted her chin and managed a smile in return. "I know it is. They were idiots not to award me the money."

Judith gave her a nod. "We'll draw up the papers. Do everything properly. And it will give me an excuse to get out of this godforsaken gown after all."

"I suggest a work dress," Daisy intoned, "of sheerest lace and rubies."

Judith grinned at her. "Of course. We shall accept nothing less."

rash had tried to make his way to the stage immediately, but Daisy had disappeared in the congratulatory throng that surrounded Mr. Flisk after the competition came to an end.

He'd given up trying to reach her after three minutes attempting to elbow well-wishers aside. The absence of Daisy fed his ire. Didn't any of these idiots know that Daisy ought to have won? Did they not care that the grocer making the award had purposefully humiliated her during what should have been a moment of celebration? That the entire thing was a cruel travesty?

Every congratulatory remark that he heard felt like coals heaped on his head.

Finally, afraid of losing his temper, he backed away from the entire mass of idiots and waited. He waited while the happy cluster of friends and acquaintances slowly dissipated, watching every person who pulled away from that tight, crowded knot, one by one.

After fifteen minutes, it was clear that she had escaped by some other route. He left the square with a quick, sure stride. But she wasn't on the street outside, conversing with any of the other folk. She wasn't around the corner. She wasn't at her flower shop. He tried first one park, then the other, the footpath by the canal, the river walk, her own home, his rooms, and then, just in case he'd missed her, all those locations once again.

He ended up at his aunt's flat. Daisy had gone there once. Maybe she had visited again.

Merry voices rang from inside; they stopped all at once at the sound of his knock.

His aunt answered the door a minute later. She frowned at him.

"Crash. What are you doing here? It's whist night."

"Is, ah, is…" He trailed off.

He'd expected to see the usual three women here, playing alongside the little pencil sketch of Martha Claving. But Martha's picture had been moved to the mantel. Now there were four women.

The fourth was Daisy's mother.

"Ah." He blinked, unsure of what he was seeing. "Mrs. Whitlaw. Um. Is your daughter…"

His aunt just shook her head. "No, Crash, she isn't here. We thought she was with you."

He didn't know what these women were doing together. Why were they discussing him and Daisy? *He* had barely discussed the matter with Daisy.

"Where's the rum?" Harriet asked.

"I don't have—"

"Hmm." She sniffed. "No rum, no entrance."

His aunt barred the door.

"Also, no Daisy, no entrance. What are you doing?"

"What am *I* doing?" He threw up his hands in bafflement. "What are the lot of *you* doing?"

Behind him, Daisy's mother rolled her eyes. "What does it look like they're doing? They're teaching me how to cheat at cards."

His aunt made a shooing motion. "Get out. Go away. We don't need you."

Crash refused to give up; he just needed to regroup. He made his way home, up the stairs to his rooms. He came to the final landing and stopped.

Daisy sat just outside his door, looking as tired as he felt. She huddled on the floor, her arms around her knees. She looked up at him with wide, hurt eyes. Then she smiled.

His heart lifted. His weariness fell away. "Daisy, what are you doing here?"

She met his eyes and slowly—not entirely gracefully—clambered to her feet. "Where have you been?"

"Looking for you." He set his hand against the wall next to her. "Where have you been?"

"Waiting for you." She gave him a smile. A bright one. A brilliant one, in fact, one that warmed him everywhere.

"No," he said. "Never mind any of that. How are you, Daisy? That stage—what happened this morning has been much on my mind. I saw your face. I saw what they did to you." He took a step toward her. "I wish I had a host of well-fed pigeons to release over their heads. How are you?"

"Truly?" She took a step toward him. "I feel bruised. Hurt. Angry. Sad."

"Of course you do." Then, because she stood mere inches from him, he reached out to her. He cupped her cheek with his fingers, stroking the soft warmth of her skin. "Of course you do."

"I am also," Daisy said, "determined, triumphant, and exuberant. They won't stop me."

There was something in her eyes as she spoke. Something so strong and unbreakable that he wanted to squeeze her tight, just to prove that she was real. "Of course they won't."

"They can't," she said. "They handed me the largest pile of dung a horse has ever dropped on the street and pretended it was my due. That I deserved nothing better." Her chin went up in defiance. "I held it. I *smelled* it. And I'm throwing it back at them." Her eyes bored into his. "When you feel your velocipede slipping, there's only one thing to do."

"Go faster," he said softly.

"Don't stop. Go hard. Pedal. Don't flinch. Maybe you'll still fall, but maybe, just maybe, you'll make it through the other end." Her smile glittered. "I've signed partnership papers. With Lady Ashworth—that's Judith."

He grinned at her. "Have you now?"

"I have. And I was thinking. You told me a while back that you'd looked at a storefront that was too large by half."

"Yes?"

"If you haven't committed to anything yet… Do you suppose we might take it together? We could divide the space in two."

He broke out in a grin. "Yes, Daisy. I think we might. I rather think we might." He paused. "You know, it wasn't just space for a business. There were living quarters above the shop."

"Oh." She looked over at him and a small smile touched her face. "Oh dear. We shall have to argue over who gets them. And I had so hoped that we were done with arguing."

He folded his arms. Two could play at that game. "No arguing necessary. We shall simply divide them down the middle."

"What a lovely solution," Daisy said. "Be sure to tell me which half is yours so I can come visit. I've been told you have scones. And tea. And orgasms."

"God, Daisy." He found himself laughing. "I love you. Will you please stop teasing me and tell me you'll marry me and share everything?"

"I suppose if there are pastries…" She hesitated just a moment. "Then, yes. Yes. I might as well admit that I love you, too."

Their hands clasped. She leaned toward him.

"Wait." He stopped her. How he stopped her when she was on the verge of kissing him, when her lips were so close he could have touched them with his tongue, he didn't know. "Wait. I have some bad news about your mother."

She gasped. "Oh, God. My mother. Is she… Has anything happened?"

He shook his head sadly at her. "You'll never beat her at whist again. My aunt has found her out. She cheats, and she'll teach your mother *everything.*"

Daisy smiled. "Good. My mother could use a little cheating in her life."

Ever so slowly, he wound his arms around her.

"So can I," he said.

Her lips brushed his, and he pulled her to him.

Epilogue

Four months later

There ought to have been some sort of fanfare. Daisy would have settled for a single trumpet playing a few triumphant notes. After months of hard work, the world ought to have announced the alteration of Daisy's life with something more than the chiming of a church bell two streets away.

That was all she had, though. Daisy turned the iron key in the lock on a sunny spring morning and opened the door to her new emporium. The key didn't even give so much as a portentous squeak.

The door swung open onto the cobblestone street. The glass window showcasing Daisy's goods glittered in the sunlight.

It was just another day. Soon this would be prosaic. Daisy danced a little jig of excitement in place and retreated back inside.

Nothing to do now but wait for customers.

Daisy was too nervous to sit. She paced instead— from one end of the store to the other. The mahogany chairs in the sitting area for tea and biscuits gleamed with polish, but she wiped them down anyway. The brightly colored scarves didn't need to be rearranged, but she fussed with them regardless.

That all took precisely one minute.

She glanced out the window, and the bell on the door rang.

In came Mrs. Wilde. In the months since the competition, they'd conversed several times. Daisy had promised her that if she ever needed an assistant, she would ask her first.

The woman looked around and smiled.

"My dear, this is lovely. You've done an excellent job."

Daisy smiled in pleasure.

"I'm here for my buttonhole," Mrs. Wilde said. "Then I'll be out of your hair. I'm sure you'll be busy."

Daisy hoped so. "Flowers. Excellent. We've three choices today. Violets, nasturtiums, and—"

The bell rang again, and Daisy looked up. She didn't recognize the woman who came in. She wore a light green gown with a gold sash, and she smiled and looked about with an air of satisfaction.

"Good day," Daisy started.

But a man entered ten seconds behind her, and Daisy *did* recognize him. He was one of the judges from the competition. The last one, the one who had chosen Daisy to give her presentation. He had set her up for that painful embarrassment.

Daisy winced. She'd be gracious. She *would*. She prepared a smile, however false it was.

"You were right, Benjamin." The woman turned to the man behind her. "She *has* done an excellent job."

Daisy inhaled in surprise.

"Let me look at these hairpieces," the woman said, and the couple walked across the room.

Daisy turned back to Mrs. Wilde. "And tulips," she finished in a voice scarcely above a whisper.

Her mind had not yet recovered from the shock. The judge had thought she would do an excellent job?

She wasn't sure how to credit it.

But after Mrs. Wilde had left with a cluster of tulips, the woman in the green frock picked out a bangle, a set of hairpins with paste jewels on them, and a scarf. Her husband paid for them, counting exact change from a coin purse.

"Thank you," Daisy said.

He met Daisy's eyes. "I voted for your proposal at the end."

She blinked.

He shrugged. "Scant comfort, I imagine, to know the final tally was one against four. But if you want that comfort, there it is."

The bell rang as Daisy stared in stunned confusion. "Thank you," she managed. "And thank you for your patronage."

She didn't have time to say more. The bell rang yet again, and soon her emporium was flooded with customers. The class on dressing hair as a single woman without assistance was filled by eleven; she added an additional day, and *that* was filled by noon. She had to replenish the bangles from the store she kept in the back twice, the scarves three times, and the hairpins... Lord, she'd need to order more of those the minute she had a chance.

If this kept up, she would need to hire a shop girl. She'd need two.

At ten minutes from closing, the shop was still full. She scarcely looked when the bell rang again.

She saw a man removing a dark hat, a flash of auburn hair. The man was holding a young girl's hand. The child smiled brightly at Daisy, her red hair a cloud of curls around her.

"Can I—" the girl started.

Daisy recognized her; she'd been sitting on her father's lap during the competition.

"Go ahead, pumpkin." The man released her hand. He didn't look at Daisy.

But he accompanied his daughter to the register when she returned in five minutes. The little girl placed a bracelet of wooden beads on the counter.

"Two pence, please."

Her father set two pennies down and looked directly at Daisy. "I wasn't sure about you then. But my daughter was at the competition, and she's been asking me to go to your store." He trailed off, frowning. "I'm *still* not sure."

"Enjoy the bracelet," Daisy said to the young girl. "We'll have new ones in next week, so be sure to stop by."

Her father let out a sigh.

"I will!" promised the child. "Papa, look at my wrist."

"I see it, poppet. It's very pretty. Just like the rest of you."

He was the last to leave, and as Daisy locked the door behind him and drew the curtains, she wanted to laugh triumphantly. She wanted to waltz around the room. And she would, right after she collapsed to the floor in a puddle of weariness.

Footsteps sounded behind her. Then a voice spoke in low tones.

"I believe I promised that you would have tea and pastries, madam."

Daisy turned.

Crash stood behind her. He'd come in through the back door that joined their two shops. He had a tray, one stocked with sandwiches and some biscuits that he must have set aside from her store earlier, because she'd been positive there was nothing left but crumbs.

"I tried to bring you something at eleven," he said, "but you were busy. So…" He set the tray down in her sitting area and waved her to a seat. "Sit."

She did. "How was your day?" Crash had opened his velocipede store over a month ago.

He didn't sit beside her. He knelt in front of her on the floor and very gently removed a slipper. His fingers pressed into the ball of her foot, into sore flesh that had been abused all day. She let out a little moan.

He shrugged. "Delightful. The appointment system you came up with last week has cut down the worst of the arguments. Who knew that the velocipede would prove so popular? One would have to be a downright genius to foresee that."

She took a sandwich and bit into it. She was hungry, and his fingers were pulling all the aches from her feet, her calves.

"*You* foresaw that," she pointed out. "You did."

He looked up at her with a glitter in his eyes. "Ah. So I did. In fact, I suppose my genius is matched only by that of someone who recognized the need for a store catering to working-class women."

"Ah." Daisy smiled. The shop needed to be swept, the shelves restocked, new goods ordered, and the books done… She would never sleep. "Yes. My genius is much overtaxed at the moment."

"I'm greatly pleased," Crash said, moving his hands up stockinged feet, "that my wife is also a genius. There's wine upstairs and dinner."

Daisy sighed. "After. I still have to—"

Crash shook his head. "When I saw how busy you were, I asked Cecilia Evans to come by in fifteen minutes. She'll clean and restock, and you can eat dinner."

"Eat dinner." Daisy smiled at him. "Is *that* what we're calling it these days? You didn't just promise me tea and pastries."

"So I didn't. I know what else you need."

Daisy waited.

"You'll need a good night's sleep." His tone was pious. His look—and the touch of his hand against her knee—was utterly wicked.

"Hmm." She considered him. "Do you know what helps me sleep?"

His smile broadened. "Yes," he said. "Now that you mention it? Yes, I do."

Thank you!

Thank you for reading *Her Every Wish*. I hope you enjoyed it.

So what happens with everyone else in the Worth family?

Her Every Wish is a side story in the Worth Saga. The Worth Saga is a story about the Worth family—Judith, Benedict, Camilla, Theresa, Anthony, and some others you haven't yet met.

If you haven't read Judith's story yet, it's available as *Once Upon a Marquess*.

If you want to know when the next book in the Worth Saga will be out, please sign up for my new release e-mail list at http://www.courtneymilan.com.

What can you tell me about the next book?

Next up is *After the Wedding*. Camilla Worth and Adrian Hunter will cross paths, and sparks will fly.

What do you mean *others you haven't yet met*?

There are seven full-length books in the series. The Worth Saga is, of course, a series about the Worth family. But it's also a series about an organization (which you'll first discover in Book 3, *The Devil Comes Courting*) and another family (which you'll meet for the first time in Book 2, *After the Wedding*). And, as with all my series, there will be a handful of novellas that explore side characters.

You can read an excerpt from Camilla's book right after this page.

When will all these books release?

I'm not a fast writer, unfortunately, and I'm extremely bad at predicting when I'm going to finish a book. At my best guess, maybe late in 2016 for Camilla's book? Add question marks to the end of any date I ever give you. Add lots of question marks. If you want to get an email when my books become available, you can sign up for my new release e-mail list at www.courtneymilan.com. Or you can follow me on twitter at @courtneymilan, or like my Facebook page at http://facebook.com/courtneymilanauthor.

I don't want to wait that long! What can I do in the meantime?

I have three other finished historical romance series (as well as a handful of stories that aren't in any series). If you're new to my books, I suggest starting The Brothers Sinister Series with *The Duchess War*. It's free on most platforms right now. It's the first book in the Brothers Sinister series, and it's about Robert Blaisdell, the Duke of Clermont, who doesn't want to be a duke, and Minnie the shy wallflower who doesn't want to be a duchess.

After that, you might want to read The Turner Series and The Carhart Series.

If you haven't tried it yet, I also have a contemporary romance series. *Trade Me* is the first book in the series. It has all the things you know and love about Courtney Milan books (humor, angst, and lengthy author's notes about things I couldn't stop researching), but there are bonus smartwatches. Come for the technology; stay for foul-mouthed billionaires and jokes about insider trading.

If you've already read all my books, I have a list of recommendations for other authors on my website at http://www.courtneymilan.com.

After the Wedding: Excerpt

Adrian Hunter has concealed his identity and posed as a servant to assist his powerful uncle. He's on the verge of obtaining the information he needs when circumstances spiral out of his control. He's caught alone with a woman he scarcely knows. When they're discovered in this compromising circumstance, he's forced to marry her at gunpoint. Luckily, his uncle should be able to obtain an annulment. All Adrian has to do is complete his mission…and not consummate the marriage, no matter how enticing the bride may be.

Lady Camilla Worth has never expected much out of life—not since her father was convicted of treason and she was passed from family to family. A marriage, no matter how unfortunate the circumstances under which it was contracted, should mean stability. It's unfortunate that her groom doesn't agree. But Camilla has made the best of worse circumstances. She is determined to make her marriage work. All she has to do is seduce her reluctant husband.

From Chapter One

ady Camilla Worth had dreamed of marriage ever since she was twelve years of age.

It didn't have to be marriage. It didn't have to be romantic. Sometimes she imagined that one of the girls whose acquaintance she made—however briefly—would become her devoted friend, and they would swear a lifelong loyalty to one another. She'd daydreamed when she lived in Leeds about becoming a companion—no, an almost-granddaughter—to an elderly woman who lived three houses down.

"What would I ever do without you, Camilla?" old Mrs. Marsdell would say as Camilla wormed her way into her heart.

But Old Mrs. Marsdell never stopped frowning at her suspiciously, and Camilla had been packed up and shunted off to another family long before she'd had a chance to charm anyone.

That was all she had ever wanted. One person, just one, who promised not to leave her. She didn't need love. She didn't need wealth. After nine times packing her bags and boarding trains, braving swaying carts, or even once, walking seven miles with her aging valise in tow… After nine separate families, she would have settled for tolerance and a promise that she would always have a place to stay.

So of course she hoped for marriage. Not the way she might have as a child, dreaming of white knights and houses to look over and china and linen to purchase. She hoped for it in the most basic possible terms.

All she wanted was for someone to choose her.

Hoping for so little, she had believed that surely she could not be disappointed.

It just went to show. Fate had a sense of humor, and she was a capricious bitch.

For here Camilla stood on her wedding day. Wedding night, really. Her gown was not white, as Victoria's had been. In fact, she was still wearing the apron from the scullery. She had no waiting trousseau, no idea what sort of home—if any—awaited her. And she'd still managed to miss out on her dreams.

Her groom's face was hidden in the shadows; late as this wedding was, on this particular night, a few candles lit in the nave did more to cast shadows than shed illumination. He adjusted his cuffs, gleaming white against the brown of his skin, and folded his arms in disapproval. She couldn't see his eyes in the darkness, but his eyebrows made grim lines of unhappy resignation.

It might even have been romantic—for versions of *romantic* that conflated *foolhardy* with *fun*—to marry a man she had known for only three days. And what she knew of the groom was not terrible. He'd been kind to her. He had made her laugh. He had even—once—touched her hand and made her heart flutter.

It might have been romantic, but for one tiny little thing.

"Adrian Hunter," Bishop Cantrell was saying. "Do you take Camilla Worth to be your wife? Will you love her, comfort her, honor and protect her, and forsaking all others, be faithful to her as long as you both shall live?"

She would have overlooked the gown, the trousseau, anything. Anything but...

"No," said her groom. "I do not consent to this."

That one tiny little thing. Like everyone else in the world, her intended didn't want her.

Behind him, Rector Daniels lifted the pistol. His hands gleamed white on the barrel in the candlelight, like maggots writhing on tarnished steel.

"It doesn't matter what you say," the man said. "You will agree and you will sign the book, damn your eyes."

"I do this under duress." His words came out clipped and harsh. "I do not consent."

Camilla shouldn't even call him her intended. *Intent* on his part was woefully lacking.

"I'm sorry," Camilla whispered.

He didn't hear her. Maybe he didn't care.

She wouldn't have minded if he didn't love her. She didn't want white lace and wedding cake. But this wasn't a marriage, not really. She was being wrapped up like an unwanted package again and sent on to the next unsuspecting soul.

After being passed on—and on—and on—and on— after all these years, she had no illusions about the outcome in this case.

The candlelight made Mr. Hunter's features seem even darker than they had in the sun. In the sun, after all, he'd smiled at her.

He didn't smile now.

There it was. Camilla was getting married, and her husband didn't want her.

Her lungs felt too small. Her hands were shaking. Her corset wasn't even laced tightly, but still she couldn't seem to breathe. Little green spots appeared before her eyes. Dancing, whirling.

Don't faint, Camilla, she admonished herself. *Don't faint. If you faint, he might leave you behind, and then where will you be?*

She didn't faint. She breathed. She said yes, and the spots went away. She managed not to swoon on her way to sign the register. She did everything except look at the unwilling groom whose life had so forcibly been tied to her own.

She followed him out into the cold winter evening. There would be no celebration, no dinner. Behind her back, she heard the clink of coins as the bishop turned to Mr. Hunter.

"There's an inn a mile away," the man said. "They might allow you to take rooms for the night. Don't expect that I'll give you a character reference."

Mr. Hunter made no response. He just started walking down the road.

That was how Camilla left the tenth family that had taken her in: on foot, at eleven at night, with a chill in the air and the moon high overhead. She had to half-skip to keep up with her new…husband? Should she call him a husband?

His long legs ate away at the ground. He didn't look at her.

But halfway to the inn, he stopped. At first, she thought he might finally address her. Instead, he let his own satchel fall to the ground. He looked up at the moon.

His hands made fists at his side. "Fuck." He spoke softly enough that she likely wasn't supposed to hear that epithet.

"Mr. Hunter?"

He turned to her. She still couldn't see his eyes, but she could feel them on her. He'd lost his position and gained a wife, all in the space of a few hours. She didn't imagine that he was happy with her.

He exhaled. "I suppose this…is what it is. We'll figure this mess out in the morning."

The morning. After the wedding came the wedding night. Camilla wasn't naïve. She just wasn't ready.

How had her life come to this?

Ah, yes. It had started three days ago, when Bishop Cantrell had arrived on her doorstep with Mr. Hunter in tow…

After the Wedding will be out in late 2016.

Other Books by Courtney

Talk Sweetly to Me

The Turner Series
Unveiled
Unlocked
Unclaimed
Unraveled

Not in any series
A Right Honorable Gentleman
What Happened at Midnight
The Lady Always Wins

The Carhart Series
This Wicked Gift
Proof by Seduction
Trial by Desire

Author's Note

I had the initial idea for this book a long time ago—in 2011, when I was doing research for *The Duchess War*. I ran into a bit of something in the Leicester archives advertising a charity loan for young residents of the parish looking to start a new trade or business. I remember reading the language very carefully and thinking to myself, huh. They don't say you have to be a man to apply.

I thought I knew precisely what to do with that. Except the problem was finding an appropriate hero. I tried someone who was in the competition against Daisy, but unfortunately, didn't like that dynamic. I tried one of the judges. I tried someone who was tasked with persuading her to withdraw. None of those things worked for me for a number of reasons.

And then, when I was writing, *Once Upon a Marquess*, a random minor character appeared on the screen and I called him Crash. I don't know why. It's not exactly a name one would normally use. But as soon as I wrote the name—Crash—I figured out that his real name was Nigel, and everything sort of followed from there.

The word "bicycle" was in use back in 1866, although rarely; I've chosen to use the word "velocipede" almost exclusively because the velocipedes of 1866 were dissimilar from today's bicycles in a number of ways. For one, there was no bicycle chain in most production models. There were definitely no shocks. And bicycle helmets are an incredibly recent invention. Nonetheless, the bicycle was an amazing invention, and it became all the rage late in the 1860s. Crash would have been perfectly positioned to take over the craze.

Britain was an empire, and for a very long time, one of the chief products that empire sought after was labor. It was involved in the African slave trade for a very long time, until slavery was outlawed in Britain itself in 1772, followed by the abolition of the trade in slaves in 1807, and finally by slavery in British colonies in 1833. This did not end the thirst for cheap labor. In lieu of African slaves, Britain would impress sailors (both domestically and internationally). It was one of the global players engaged in what was colloquially known as the "pig trade"—which involved Chinese laborers who were indentured servants, where some of them entered their period of servitude more involuntarily than others. And of course, Britain ruled over numerous colonies where cheap, abundant, exploitable labor was used—India being one of them.

These workers were often impressed into doing grunt work for the merchant marines. As you can imagine, worker safety was not highly valued, and workers who were injured on the job back in those days had little by way of regulatory protection. The global empire of Britain is littered with stories of sailors from around the world being marooned in various ports. If they weren't able to work to the rigorous standards of an ocean-going vessel, they might find themselves far from home with no way to return.

Britain didn't obtain racial data in its census for quite some time, and so reconstructing questions like how many people of color were in Britain in the latter half of the nineteenth century is difficult. But how many is not relevant to the question of their general existence: They were absolutely there, and it's probably reasonable to assume that those who ended up in London for one reason or another tended to band together.

When I was doing research for Talk Sweetly to Me, I read an essay about how a photographer in the 1920s who was taking pictures of working-class people discovered a tiny neighborhood in Bristol near where the slave ships had docked over a century before. In this area, nearly everyone was some shade of brown, the result of people who had been stranded generations ago and had intermarried with each other and the local population and various sailors of every ethnicity who had wandered by.

When I wrote Crash and his aunt and their group of friends, I was imagining that sort of Bristol neighborhood in London. Given the number of people from around the world who ended up stranded in London, such a place would have to exist.

When Crash says that much of England would refer to his aunt and his friends as whores, this is not meant to be descriptive as many people would understand that term. One of the main problems that authorities had in the 1860s is that it was difficult to corral the spread of STDs because it was hard to tell who was involved in sex work and who wasn't. This is in part because upper-class English gentlemen were jerks who thought they could have sex with anyone poor, and in part because prostitution just didn't work the way they thought it did. There were some people who only earned a living in prostitution, but a huge number of people who might be classified as sex workers back then had a regular job, and then maybe a man or three on the side. Many authorities basically assumed that anyone working jobs that earned little enough money had to be involved in prostitution on the side.

Finally, a note on two items mentioned in the book. The velocipede really did start to become popular at the end of the 1860s, and it has basically never stopped since, despite significant advancements in transportation technology. Crash would have gotten his foot in the door right at the start. Crash is also (basically) right when he says that you're more stable on a bicycle the faster you go. For the same reason, tops wobble less when you spin them faster. It's a physical phenomenon known as precession. I didn't want to go into too much detail, because obviously the faster you go, the more you can hurt yourself, and bicycle helmets were a shockingly recent invention, compared to the history of the bicycle.

Second, there is such a thing as a carbolic smoke ball, and that (like other random things that show up in my book) is a joke between me and ten thousand law students who will all say, "ARGH, CARBOLIC SMOKE BALLS!" There's a famous case from 1892 involving an advertisement for a carbolic smoke ball.

The basic idea behind a carbolic smoke ball was that the ball contained carbolic acid, which interacted with the air and filtered it. The makers of the ball claimed it would filter out, say, influenza germs. Like about 95% of the purveyors of Victorian-era medical equipment, they were totally wrong. The actual Carbolic Smoke Ball Company featured in the 1892 advertisement didn't exist in 1866, but upon research, I did find references to early inventions that were basically carbolic smoke balls that were period. So I hope you enjoy it.

Acknowledgments

Thank you to Lindsey Faber, Rawles Lumumba, Wendy Chan, and Louisa Jordan for reading this novella on short notice.

Thanks to Melissa Jolly for everything she does.

Beyond that, thanks to everyone in my life who keeps me going: my husband, Carey, my dog, Pele, my cat, Silver, and my chickens, Iphigenia and Bob, who have finally started to produce eggs (thank you!). My friends are too numerous to name, but Tessa Dare, Carey Baldwin, Brenna Aubrey, Alisha Rai, Bree Bridges, Rebekah Weatherspoon, Alyssa Cole, and Leigh LaValle have also provided untold emotional support.

Finally, an extremely belated thanks to Apple. Yes, that Apple. It's not exactly a secret that I'm an Apple fangirl, but I've written every book I've ever produced on Apple products. I really appreciate it.

2015 and 2016 have also been weird writing years for me. I suspect it looks like my writing has slowed down from prior years. The truth is that I've actually been writing a lot of things concurrently.

So finally, to all of you… Thank you for reading. Thank you for your patience. I hope it will be rewarded…soonish, and that you'll think that it has been worth the wait.